Chromotherapy

Jarron Blake

Published by Jarron Blake, 2024.

This is a work of fiction. Similarities to real people, places, or events are entirely coincidental.

CHROMOTHERAPY

First edition. July 4, 2024.

Copyright © 2024 Jarron Blake.

ISBN: 979-8224130566

Written by Jarron Blake.

Table of Contents

Death.. 1

Friendship 14

Freedom of Speech 29

Religion 40

Mental Health 65

Identity 77

Life..101

Afterword..108

For my grandmother Loretta and my grandfather
Jerry

I wish I could have shared more stories with you.

And For My grandmother Gussie

Thank you for everything

Cogito, ergo sum,
"I think, therefore I am"
- René Descartes. 1641

A man said to the universe:
"Sir, I exist!"
"However," replied the universe,
"The fact has not created in me
A sense of obligation."
-Stephen Crane, 1899

Preface

My inner voice never shuts up.

I'm sure most people who have been dubbed the "quiet kid" can relate. One day I just stopped talking to people. I didn't feel the need to engage, I just wanted to listen. That doesn't mean I had nothing to say, I just kept my mouth shut. I found a power in the prison of silence. I got used to the hypothetical shower arguments and epic fantasies of telling off bullies in front of the whole school. I slowly felt myself feeling nothing in the moment and screaming my feelings later when I was alone. I could blame it on depression or a bad childhood, but I don't know if it matters. I would like to think I'm better at talking now. The imaginary me inside my head seems to think so.

As someone always listening, I've always been fascinated by the things people don't say. Someone can say something to me in private, but when the person they were just talking about comes around, they sing a different song. People sugarcoat bitter pills, that way you don't associate them with negativity. In effort to save feelings we as a society deemed that honesty isn't always what a person needs despite it being "the best policy". You can't say you hate Fiona's hand knitted sweater she made for you, even if it's too small and there's no head hole; you are not allowed to tell Bill that you think his man cave is creepy and you're now worried about him in every way; you can't tell Ramon that you don't know if you're strong enough to survive another holiday with the family. This aspect of the society I participate in has always been a burden to me. I don't doubt many can relate, just as I don't doubt many still participate; *I* still participate. Just as I ponder the thoughts I can see on people's faces (if they don't outright tell me) that they don't say, I do the same with my own. I retreat into myself.

I usually tell people when they ask me a question with any amount of weight to it that I want to choose my words carefully. Most people think I mean I'm finding the right words to be polite, but more often than not I'm choosing which road of thoughts am I going with. I don't see one perspective as I'm not locked into one feeling all the time. It's hard sometimes to cut through the thick fog of feeling worthless and hopeless, but underneath is a person who wants to be understood. They want that understanding from the person they're speaking to, almost as much as they want to understand themselves. Understanding why I feel the need to just pause and think before answering would always make me think of myself as a character to be studied. What is the deep lore that has made this person the way they are? Where is this darkness coming from? Then I try to think of literally anything else because the darkness scares me. It scares me because I can't see the end to it, I can't even begin to perceive its depth and before I know it, I go from thinking about it to already stuck in it.

The darkness chokes; the darkness keeps you down under it; the darkness makes you thrash and push those that want to help you away. As you drift and sink, you stop fighting. It starts to feel correct to not fight it. You think, *do I deserve this?* No, of course not. You know that, but it's hard to even believe yourself. Depression is a raggedy bitch. That said, I'm obsessed with how it makes me think. I wish I could give you a more positive note to dive into the story with, but I can't say the story you're about to ready isn't a sweet fantasy.

If you're willing, I'm welcoming you to explore my madness.

Death

***

What would you say if I told you that you were talking to a dead man? No, this isn't a ghost tale, and I'm not a sentient zombie. You can stop wracking your brain trying to figure me out because I'll just tell you: I'm simply just dead and forgotten already. I'm, of course, referring to the future, a time when we'll all be gone. Remember that "forever" is just a fantasy. Something that frames humanity in a way that I find unwaveringly true is that we are starlight. Dead symbols that most people don't see until the body that the symbol represents is gone. The stars that we see are already dead.

It takes far too long for the light a star radiates to reach our eyes. What we are actually seeing is how the stars were centuries ago. We only have value in death when we need to give the ones left behind something to point at and say, "how beautiful" and make them think about their life. Our "value" is inspiring unearned value in someone else and their dreams. So naturally, following this logic: we're all dead, we're all meaningless, congratulations.

So please, don't tell me trite things like my friend died before his time. How can it be "before his time" and "everything happens for a reason" simultaneously? Don't tell me that I'm risking my life unnecessarily just because I'm doing something that you don't have the stones to do; I'm quite aware of the risk. You wouldn't tell me that ineffectual malarkey when I'm about to walk down a dark street alone. You wouldn't tell me that when I am about to board a bus with an elderly driver. You don't say that when I go home to sit in a dark room alone with a laptop for light and my dark thoughts. You don't tell me that when I browse social media, hoping to come out happier. You don't tell me that when I just choose to exist.

Don't tell me that my "self-destructive tendencies" make you feel x, y, or even, and especially that dirty bastard of a letter z. I do not care, and neither do you. We could talk for hours and hours until I say that "we all matter." I could tell you that "I matter and deserve happiness." I could tell you, "I'm okay, and you really inspired me." I can tell you that I am stronger now because of the cliché phrases you memorized from movies and television. I can tell you that just you talking at me and... "setting me straight" with your tough love got to me, and I know the future is bright. I could hold back the urge to vomit and tell you all of the pretty phrases humans have come up with. There's just no point to any of that. Why delay or fight what was already predetermined? Your picking and choosing on what you hold value in just contradicts my picking and choosing. The second that you are born, you start to die, so why live?

***

"Are you okay? Hey! Get up. We have to go!" I heard a voice say. It sounded so familiar. *It sounded screechy.* Just as I thought that, I realized I couldn't recall where I was. My brain couldn't open my eyes for some reason. I tried, but it was like I was telling someone else's sleeping body to wake up, and they couldn't hear me.

Wherever I was, it was cold. I felt my body lying down on hard pavement. I could hear explosions around me. My body was showered in rushes of chilly wind, and the air in my ears was both deafening and stinging. If the cold wasn't bad enough to breathe in, the smell of something foul burning in the air choked me. Despite that, I heard people shouting. When I forced myself to listen, it sounded more like one person shouting in different voices. The inside of my head felt as if my thoughts had become material, jagged, and were scrambling around.

"Hey! Wake up," the voice said again, or did I say that? It sounded so close to my inner thoughts, but I think someone said it.

I commanded my eyes to open and saw a person looking down on me. He was a man with brown skin, a thin black beard, and a head of short but thicker curly hair. There were round features throughout his face, and he had a round, stocky body. His voice was deep but a little squeaky, but there was a light bounce to it. It was like a sweet melody. He wore a pink shirt with a yellow star under a white opened button down with black shoulders and buttons. He also had silver jeans and black running shoes.

I took notice but couldn't tell if this was strange or not, but the color of his eyes was pink. I still don't know what about that I would find strange, and that to me seems concerning. I thought it was stranger that his face expressed worry that I couldn't fully comprehend. Then, I suddenly remembered that I was on the ground. That triggered a sudden, big gulp of ashy air into my lungs. When I let that air back out, I could suddenly feel aware of my body; I felt it relax and I didn't find that relaxing.

"Thank goodness," the man said with a sigh. The wind and explosions suddenly fell silent. I looked around. There were no signs of explosions. Just a drab and dusty scene. There were shops all around with dark gray "open" signs, but the buildings were either light gray or tan, except for a pink and black building with a spinning red, white, and blue striped pole. I looked down, and the gray ground had splotches of pink chalk drawings partially covered by patches of black dust. There were spurts of green grass popping up and full patches outside the pink building. I didn't know where I was. I felt a hand on my forehead, and I was snapped back to the stranger over me.

"Who are you?" I asked, shocking myself that I knew how to speak. Honestly, if I wasn't looking at his face, I would have thought the stranger would have said it.

"My name is Quartz. Who are *you*?" he asked slowly. I thought about it, but I couldn't answer him. "It's okay," he said with a warm smile and a pat on my shoulder. "Cerulean!" he called. "We got a live one over here."

"A live *what*?" a voice angrily asked. It sounded almost like Quartz but angrier. I only knew it wasn't him because, at this point, I was just staring at him.

"Did you take care of the—" Quartz started to say.

"I get shit done fast, in case you haven't noticed," the angry voice said. I don't waste energy on *Greens*."

"It's our job to protect Greens," Quartz said, looking at me. "They're never a waste."

"They're practically dead from the start. Why should we go down with them?"

"Enough, Merlot. Do your job. He's still weak. I think he might have just landed."

"I hate existing," the angry man, apparently named Merlot, sighed. I felt two big hands pick me up under my arms, and I was tossed over a shoulder in a quick motion. As I was there, I could hear Quartz talking about being gentle. All I could see what the back of someone, *a really big back.* I could see that they were wearing a dark red T-shirt, black jeans, and black shoes. It was very uncomfortable, but something in me told me not to protest. I lifted my head up a bit, and I saw a person in a navy-blue sweater, khaki pants, and a pair of blue and silver running shoes. I couldn't see their face. Someone else was here.

"Where's Gold?" Quartz asked.

"Surveying," a voice said. It also sounded like Quartz, but a little more bored and sophisticated, or stuck up, depending on how you look at it. *Hear at it?*

"Oh, now you pipe up?" Merlot asked. I guess his voice is just permanently angry and rough.

"I've learned that it's best to let you all hash it out before I give any input."

"Coward."

"Stop it, Merlot," Quartz said. "You were saying Cerulean?"

"Greens may already be dead, but so are the rest of us. We exist, but the fact has not created in this universe a sense of obligation. Let's just take him to Inverno. We shouldn't burden ourselves for nothing."

***

That's another thing, *burden*. Why are we all so keen on continuing this existence? Why would you bring someone into this world and then complain about the costs of raising them, the personal sacrifices, and the worry? Shuttle them off to schools. Expose them to disease. Have their world view shatter, then help them pick up the pieces. Then you shatter what you built together because the foundation was flimsy lies made of shards of forced trust. They have to look for someone else's help to rebuild, and you judge what they come up with.

You judge them for who they get to help. You judge where that person comes from. You make your offspring watch you age and get sick because you had the gull to make them care about you. They try everything in their mortal power to make you feel better. Make you happy at the cost of theirs. That's if you're doing the "right thing," apparently. You make someone watch you die. Death is inevitable. But we walk around thinking that parents/guardians are permanent pillars in our lives. We know it's coming, but a part of us still hurts. Even as "rebels" who just want to not be responsible for carrying the weight of your world on our shoulders.

You make them plan and pay for a funeral for you. You probably punish them almost the entire time they're growing up. Use the excuse of not paying bills or rent in a home they never chose. Make them feel guilty, make them worry, make them scared. Again, that's doing the "right" thing? Otherwise, you just fucked someone up in the head because you're fucked up already. What the fuck is wrong with you? Why should we be subjecting anyone to this? Fucking living.

Interacting with other assholes who worm their way into your mind. Making someone feel shit. You think I want to spend the day coping with someone cutting in front of me in line? You think I want to think about what if a friend dies before me? Or when and why all of my friends betray me? What if I say the wrong thing to the wrong person and they don't return my affections? What if the skin color I didn't choose ruins someone's day, and they try to ruin my day?

What if my choice of superhero emblem to wear on a shirt offends someone? No, you never thought of that. You wanted to continue a family line. You just wanted to care for smaller versions of you. You just wanted to recreate what you had with your parents. Or some twisted version of rectifying your existence. You wanted another special parent/child time. A do-over of the first go around, you can make it all better for yourself through another person. Or you just had to keep the child because protection was too much damn work, and you feel an obligation to feed, clothe, and shelter. You just fucked, and now I'm here. Now I have to die, too. All the children will eventually die. First, their innocence dies with someone else's body, then there's death to the self, next the parent, any loved one, and finally, in actuality; with most likely a new child being roped into the mess.

Fuck you.

***

"Stop calling them nothing!" Quartz said. Funny, an angry Quartz doesn't sound like Merlot. You can really hear the sweetness in his voice, even when he's angry.

"They *are* nothing," Merlot said. "Just like the rest of us."

"We are not 'nothing.' We are fighters, we are a team of survivors, and we are all still right here."

"Even if we survive this, we're fodder. We won't live forever," Cerulean said.

"So why not just live...now?" I heard someone say. It might have been me. They were all quiet.

"Hey guys!" a cheery and zany voice that once more sounded like everyone else said. *It got more annoying.* "Woah, is that a new Green?"

"We're not keeping him," Merlot snapped.

"Awe." I heard a few footsteps. I looked up a little and saw someone getting close. They wore a bright yellow and gray checked button-down shirt over a light blue T-shirt, blue jeans, and blue and yellow running shoes. "Hey there. It's me, the face, the personality, the voice of senseless wisdom: I'm Gold."

I lifted my head up a little more and choked on a gasp. This man had the same face as Quartz but with yellow eyes. I jumped and fell off the shoulder I was on. All four voices now had a body, the exact same body. They had the exact same face, just different eye colors; Pink, Yellow, Red, and Blue. I looked away from them and saw a fifth lookalike on the ground like I was. I crawled toward him; he crawled toward me, but he didn't actually seem to go anywhere. It was a large pane of broken glass that I was looking into, and green eyes staring back at me.

***

You feel that thing beating in your chest? You know what? No. I actually can't stand that stupid line. Clichés are kind of just a slap in the face sometimes. They serve a purpose, don't get me wrong, but come on. You know you have a heart; you know you're alive. So what if we're already dead in the future. We're still beautiful. We're still here now.

The stars we see in the sky aren't always dead. It's just that it's so hard to get to them before they're gone. They're farther away than they look. It feels like they're something no one would ever get to personally know in their lifetime. They float in a black void with trillions of other stars. Some are more interesting because they shine brighter or explode spectacularly or brighten up our mornings. You pray for one star to come and make your gray, dull week better. The ones you see at night are just there, not that special. So, I can see why it's easy to believe that the stars we see are dead. I can see why you feel like living doesn't matter. Maybe in the end, it doesn't.

We have the gift of choice. We can make a difference, or we can just enjoy ourselves. We can do that alone, with people who feel the same way, without hurting anyone. You shape the experience. I'd rather not live long instead of saying that I never lived at all. That I never inspired another person to live. We didn't ask to be in this world, but someone gave the gift to us. So, take it, do something special with it, leave something permanent behind. You can find value in the world's imperfections, and people can do that with you. You can lead a happy life. You'll always be enough, so there's no way you can be worthless.

You're here. With me, with friends, even the ones you haven't made yet, family, even the ones you haven't chosen yet, people you don't even know you've touched. You're here with yourself. It's never too late to live, to laugh, to *shine*. Shine so bright that you're blinding. So bright that years from now, when they see your star, they'll wish they got to know you, thank you for being there, that maybe wish they were you.

***

"Well, that was shitty," Merlot said.

"Truly sad and terrible," Gold said flatly with a big, toothy smile. "But, oh no," he said in a more concerned tone, keeping a smile. "He's doing the "Green" thing. He's new, isn't he?"

"Yup," Merlot said. I lifted my head, and saw my image fragmented from a large break in the mirror; I could see my other reflection walking toward mine in every piece. What I was really focusing on was his hateful red eyes burning into mine. I turned toward the group of doppelgangers and scooted back away from them.

"Merlot, stop," the one with the blue eyes and bored expression said. By process of elimination, he had to be Cerulean. Merlot stopped and looked at him. "He's only going to get worse if you just grab him."

"You *mean...*" Quartz said. "He's scared, and you shouldn't terrify him more."

"Sure," Cerulean said, his eyes darting up. "In any case..."

"Who are you?" I asked. I wanted to run, but I wanted to stay. I didn't understand this.

"We're..." Gold started to say. "Uh...You'd think I'd know how to explain this by now."

"No, I really wouldn't," Cerulean said. "*In any case...*we are your guardians."

"For now," Merlot added.

"Guardians?" I asked.

"We're your own personal superhero/superspy/superfly guardian team," Gold said.

"I wish you'd stop saying that shit!" Merlot barked.

"But I'm Batman," Gold said in a gruff voice, bringing the left side of his yellow unbuttoned shirt over his face.

***

Life is short, but do you know what's shorter? My attention span.

***

"It's sort of true though," Gold continued. "We're kick-ass action stars."

"We're patsies, you idiot."

"*Proxies*," Cerulean and Quartz interjected; one said it matter-of-factly, and another said it a little more slowly and warmly.

"I MEANT WHAT I SAID!" Merlot shouted. His voice made Quartz and myself jump.

The group began to argue and tried to calm each other down at the same time. Quartz tried to get in between Merlot and Gold, who was still smiling broadly as they argued. When Merlot turned his anger on Quartz, Gold tried to jump in between those two. Then Merlot turned his anger toward Gold again, and Quartz tried to calm him again. Cerulean started to interject but stopped himself. He noticed the loop and walked off to the side. He loudly cleared his throat, but no one noticed him. I just couldn't believe what I was seeing. Four people who look like me yelling about nothing.

I started to sweat cold beads, and my stomach was in knots. I started to feel sick. But I didn't know what made me that way. I still don't really. I needed to get out of the situation. That said, I didn't have the time to process anything because someone just laid their ice-cold hand on my shoulder. I looked at it. It was glowing black and blue. Not bruised, actual glowing blue skin with large flaking black patches. It smelled like onions and rust. I turned my head slowly and saw a dense, black cloud that had a pulsing blue glow cutting through parts of it. The hand was stretched out from it. Slowly, I saw a face emerge with the same skin as on the hand, with eyes that were sunken and gray. They didn't have just any face; it was our face.

***

...

***

I wanted to scream, but I couldn't get the sound out of my mouth. I wanted to talk to this thing, but I forgot how to speak. I felt myself sinking. They weren't pushing, but I felt like I was both falling and struggling to move on the lukewarm ground. I could hear the arguing fade into incoherent mumbling. The face and hand slowly started to get more of a body as it slid out of the cloud. I felt cold all over, and it wasn't from the cold hand on me. It was radiating from my core. My blood felt like it was pooling and freezing. I couldn't breathe. I thought I was drowning. I was confused because I couldn't see water around me. I could feel water streaming down my cheeks. The air was coarse on my skin, but I still wanted it to fill my lungs. The part that scared me the most was that I didn't really care if I took another breath again. *Why don't I care? What is this?*

Friendship

Friendship is the most wonderful thing in the world! It's a connection to another person who just magically showed up in your world.

A person who you can just talk to and discover common interests.

A person who you love, and they love you back.

A person who is there at your lowest, pulling you back up even if you don't want to get up.

A person who cheers you on when you are at your highest.

A friend is a person who you want to be around, and they want to be around you.

A friend is a person who won't allow you to feel bad about yourself.

A friend never wants to hurt you.

A friend is a gift.

A gift that is a piece of your soul that you didn't even notice was missing. Cherish them, and they will cherish you. Sometimes, they do disappear, but it's always for a reason. It may be just temporary, or maybe life is just giving you space for a new friend. Maybe they're the real friend that will stay around forever after a break.

"Be careful!" Quartz called. I could only hear him because he screamed in my ear as he pulled me to the side. At the same time, Merlot was kicking the black and blue copy off me. As

Quartz dragged me away, I turned my head just in time to see Merlot stomping on the cold duplicate. In three stomps, the black and blue doppelganger let out a chilling screech and crumbled into black ash. I felt my heart stop. I didn't know what that thing was or what it was doing to me, but I knew it was bad. I knew that, but I felt sorry that he no longer existed. I felt sorry that I didn't know his name and I'll never have the chance to. I didn't think it was fair for him to have to disappear. I wanted to scream at Merlot and cry for the friend I never made all at the same time.

"I just love that their final 'screw you' is making someone have to clean that up," Gold remarked. "I mean, *I'm* not doing it, but still."

"What did you do to him?" I blurted. I looked down at my hands shaking. I think I scared myself with the concern I felt. I forced myself to stay still. I knew it was weird for that to be the first thing out of my mouth, but I stood by it. I separated from Quartz and crawled up to the ash. "What was he?"

"Nothing worth your concern," Cerulean said, stepping to the side and letting a gust of wind come and carry the ashes and what was left of the cloud away. His voice was calm, but it wasn't at all comforting. "Perhaps we should vacate the area. Even one straggler is dangerous. They can attract dozens in a matter of moments."

"Are you okay?" Quartz asked, clearly ignoring Cerulean. He stood me up and lightly brushed dirt off me with a red cloth. He paused at my hands that had ashes on them. Before I could say anything, he roughly wiped my hands clean and gave a rigid half-smile. I took a step back and looked at everyone again.

"What are you?"

***

Dude, friends are the best! You can make jokes, and they laugh even when it isn't funny. But if you get good at reading them, you can tell what really makes them smile and do useful things. You can make things together and enjoy them too. Friends keep you happy. Friends keep you creating. Friends keep you from thinking of things you may not want to be thinking. What could possibly be the downside? Maybe if they showed you their backside and you weren't ready for it. Though that could be fun in the right context I'm sure you already interpreted that statement to mean. If *we* were friends, I could think of something better for you.

***

"Irrelevant. We don't have time for this," Cerulean said slowly. I started hunching into myself, and I couldn't stop. I felt like I was being cut in half.

"Maybe we should make time," Gold said. "We're just going to make a dramatic reveal later, and by that time, everyone would have figured it out already. Or they would be so in love with their headcanon that they don't like the actual canon as much."

"What are you rambling about now?" Merlot asked.

"I'm just saying, everyone loves a trope inversion/lampshade hanging/get-on-with-it moment."

"Who would 'everyone' be?" Quartz asked. "All but one of us knows the answer." Gold just gave an exaggerated wink that didn't really seem intended for anyone here.

"Of all the asinine things..." Cerulean groaned. "This is very dull, even for me." He put a hand up toward Gold, and that cut him off from what he was about to say.

"Coming from you, that's scary," Quartz said, slapping his hands against both sides of his face. Cerulean gave a louder groan as Gold pointed at Quartz and nodded.

"Are we going or not?" Merlot asked. I would say he asked angrily, but I can't imagine him not angry at this point.

"Maybe we *should* sort this out first," Quartz asked, his words coming out slowly. His tone made me feel calmer. I felt myself stand up straight again. It felt like it was warmer inside my body.

"I just..." I felt myself say, my voice cracking. I tried folding my arms over my chest, but couldn't decide which arm should be over which, so I threw them to my sides. "I just want to know what's going on."

"Fine!" Merlot groaned. "We're guardians. It's our job to make this barren, ugly waste of space and turn into an equally ugly rainbow. Then we must take dumbass Greens like you to our asshole boss because you're too much of an idiot to not get dusted. Satisfied?"

"Who would be satisfied by that?" Gold asked. We want a Snickers, not a gumdrop."

"Shut the fuck up, Gold. You're the one who started this."

Gold gasped and placed a hand on his chest. Merlot marched up to Gold, who in turn raised his fist and bounced back and forth on his forefeet.

"I'm sorry if the same story, over and over, is boring to me, and I want a changeup. Also, how is what you said different from what I said?"

"Please calm down," Quartz said.

"I don't want to calm down!" Merlot barked.

"I know. You never want to calm down. But right now, you're not helping." Merlot stepped toward him, pointing his finger. The two locked eyes, and Merlot's finger hung in the air for a while. Merlot's face only got more and more tense. For the first time, I witnessed Quartz frowning. His eyebrows were at an angle, one hand was on his hip, he had a foot tapping. I still didn't get anger from him; it was more sad, or disappointed. Quartz reached up and put a hand on Merlot's shoulder.

As quick as it landed, Merlot shook it off and walked off to the side, folded his arms across his chest, and turned his back to us. I looked at Gold who leaned against the wall wiping his brow with a white towel and taking puffs out of an inhaler. Quartz sighed and shook his head. He turned to me and smiled. He was sweet and cheery again. "We've been tasked to bring color to this world," he said softly. "We don't know how, but we have an idea, and we're getting there. We also must make sure that you are safe. So, we take you *aaaalllll* the way over to the other side of the city," Quartz said with an exaggerated handwave. "To a friend who can help you."

"Help me what?"

"Know who you are."

"Are there a lot of... 'Greens' like me?"

"Uh..." For a second, I saw his smile fade and his eyes shift away. It was like his cheer skipped a beat. Out of the corner of my eye I could see Cerulean glaring at us. I felt a flip in my stomach. Quartz clapped his hands together and my attention snapped back to him. "I think so Champ," he said with a giggle that made me uncomfortable in its comfort. Something in the back of my mind was shouting *no*.

"But wait, the color? What do you...?" My mind went back to the pink shop from when I woke up. *More context didn't help me make sense of things.*

"Thank you, Quartz!" Gold cut in. "That's how you explain things like a Doctor Fate and not a Hulk. Hint-hint, Big Red." Cerulean gave him a confused look.

"You know what?" Merlot said, turning around quickly and advancing toward Gold, his finger extended toward his chest. He looked like he was about to say something to him when we all noticed that Cerulean was walking away. "Where the hell are you going?" Merlot called to him.

"Away from the threat that I told you *might* come and is now *coming*," Cerulean said, not stopping to turn around. We all turned, and sure enough, there was a mob of the blue and black lookalikes pouring out from a massive black cloud that covered the entire street. It was spilling toward us. I felt cold again.

"Wuh-oh, gotta go," Gold said.

"Shit," Merlot growled.

"Come on!" Quartz said. He grabbed me by the hand and without thinking, I pulled it back. I felt numb all over. Quart gave a dry laugh and grabbed me again and pulled me in the direction Cerulean was walking. We started running and passed him quickly. I looked back at him, and he seemed bored of the entire situation. Gold and Merlot rushed past him; he didn't even react.

Friends don't really make a difference. Friendship is something we have evolved to attach to the word "forever". They're just a distraction at best and a distraction at worst. You just pair up with another individual that happened to be in the same place as you. You find them when one of you decides that you are bored, and you just talk.

In the end, it will never last. They eventually get bored of you and leave your life. Or perhaps you're the bored one, or you outgrow each other. There's always that lie that you'll stay friends even if one of you moves away or changes directions. It fizzles out, or you die. Nothing lasts forever. You'll know it's the end when they make more excuses for why they're not there for you more than anything else.

If you want to go through the cycle of having someone, losing someone, learning to trust again, finding, losing, repeating, et cetera, then do it; just don't involve me. There is no point to any of it. People are sometimes great for a moment, I suppose. They start off with good intentions most of the time. It's just in time, things get more complicated and more emotional than any of it is worth. I cannot personally subscribe to such nonsense, but if it makes things quiet, I will not contest it. Find your for-the-moment and leave us that have no time for the nonsense, alone.

***

"What about Cerulean?" I asked Quartz.

"He'll catch up," Quartz said, dismissively, flicking his free hand in the air. Although he had the same face as Merlot, it was weird to see Quartz's bunched up in annoyance. He looked at me watching him and his expression immediately softened to a smile. "Which way, Gold?"

"Left!" he called from behind us. Quartz pulled me to the right, and the group ran that way. No one said anything about that, and Gold just kept smiling.

We were running through alleys of tall, dark gray buildings. None were really distinctive from another. At first, I thought it was because we were running so fast that the details were blending together around me. But the more I focused, the more time slowed down. I saw that nothing had a distinct detail other being gray. These buildings were just tall gray blocks with darker gray windows. I looked down at the dirty, light gray ground and got sad. This world is just dull. There weren't even tan buildings like the first place. It was just all nothing. I didn't know why I was getting sad. Nothing looked right and I don't even know what I mean by that. Everything was starting to blur together again. I had to focus on everyone else not to get sick.

Gold in his bright yellow shirt, Merlot in his dark clothes, Quartz standing out in pink. I looked down at my own clothes. I don't recall picking out clothes like this. A green shirt with some white leaf designs and dark blue jeans. I felt bare for some reason. *Why is everything so bleak?* I thought I said that out loud, but I didn't. I could feel that the others had the answer but probably weren't going to say anything. Before I knew it, Quartz dragged me into a building. It was dark in there. It didn't seem like anyone was trying to find a light.

"If we have to fight, stay behind us," Gold said, still sounding upbeat. I appreciated him being cheery when he said that. I don't know why. The idea of a fight with those beings was weird to me. *What isn't at this point?* "We'll beat those bullies so bad they'll see stars and canaries."

***

Friends...

***

"Why do they look like us?" I asked.

"They used to be us," I heard Cerulean say from behind us. He made me jump.

"You caught up," I said, still startled by him. When he speaks, it's like the waves of sound go into my ears and spread through my body under my skin just to personally rattle me. My stomach turns and my head pounds when I look at him and he looks through me. "I didn't see you run."

"I don't *run*," he said dismissively. I hunched in again and nodded. "I just get away from the situation."

"What did..."

"Enough fucking questions!" Merlot ordered. "They're almost here and the longer we run, the more are going to accumulate. They'll overtake us. We can't escape without a fight."

"I hope they're ready to put em' up, put em' up. I'll fight you with one paw tied behind my back," Gold said in a strange, whiny accent. He raised his hands up and started punching the air like a boxer.

"Will anything start to make sense?" I asked myself.

22

"Nope, but that's part of the fun," Gold said. It was dark, but I could tell he winked again.

"Everything makes sense, even what we perceive as nonsense," Cerulean said.

"I said no more questions!" Merlot said. "They're here." The door that we went through started to open again. I didn't realize that we had run to the back of the room. Cerulean was beside me with his arms folded across his chest. Quartz was trying to hide me behind his body.

Out in front of him, Merlot and Gold were standing side by side. Somehow, Gold had obtained boxing gloves that were almost as big as his torso and had the texture of hundreds of woven squares all over. I couldn't believe no one batted an eye at this, though in hindsight, I don't even think *I* reacted much. Their faces showed more of a wonder why he went with that than something else. Merlot stood next to him with his bare fists clenched, ready to brawl. I could feel the heat coming from him. I could also feel the entire room we were in getting colder. This was all very dizzying. My head was so cloudy I thought I could hear metal music. Merlot launched himself at the door, the battle began.

***

Friends, they have your back, or they don't. When they decide not to, and most, if not all, will, you need to be your own friend. You need to have your own back and support yourself because you know no one else will. You need to be the one to tell yourself to go for it, to fight back, to stand your ground. Because even people who you think are your friends will just hold you back and bring you down if it means that they have some company. Maybe that's all you'll ever be to a friend: company. Someone there to keep them from being bored. Maybe you're the one who has a friend so you're the one not bored. Maybe they'll use you for something they can't do themselves like fight a battle, buy what they can't afford, find something out that they're too lazy to look up. Maybe you use them back in a mutually agreed upon system of loans.

Maybe a friend is someone there to tame you. Keep you from being a danger to themselves. Maybe you do that for them, and you feel like the world makes sense. While you're using each other, you grow together and realize what you can and can't do, how your actions affect others, how you affect yourself. A friend is a mirror that reflects who you are, who you *truly* are.

A user?

A giver?

A protector?

A dominator?

A subordinate?

Whatever you are and choose to be, just make sure you don't hurt anyone. Leave people alone. Make them leave *you* alone. People aren't toys. Life's already a pain; don't try to pawn part of that burden off on someone else because you can't deal with it. Friendship shouldn't be misery and minefields.

***

I couldn't tell if it was the lack of light or not, but Merlot seemed to be gliding toward the door. He moved so fast, by the time I could formulate the thought, his fist was already connecting to the side of the head of another black and blue doppelganger. He then struck two more as they entered the room. As they fell, the clones started to crumble into dust. Merlot had a steady, slow pace of heavy blows, but this led to danger.

The black and blue copies had surrounded Merlot. He could only take on two at a time by the way he was punching them. He had a focus on slow and hard blows to the head. These "people" had sluggish movements. Their bodies hunched over, their bloodshot dark eyes straight forward like they were looking past us. Each copy seemed to be holding themselves as they walked. Some of their bodies were jerking up and down like they were wheezing or sobbing.

All I could really hear from them were grunts and choking sounds. Not much to dwell on with the choking as they didn't really start doing that until they saw Merlot and Gold were ready to fight. They were probably doing it for the attention. I instantly hated myself for thinking that. *I still do.* I felt bad for these lookalikes.

Doppelganger? Clone? Lookalike? Person? None of these felt right, but what else could I say? They all looked the same. They look like us, they look like me. But I didn't know what they were. I didn't know what I was. I still don't. All I could think was, what are they? What do they want? Why destroy them? What am I? Why—

"We call them 'Stagnant,'" Cerulean interjected. My chain of thoughts was lost. "They're nothing more than empty shells. Parasites really. All they want to do is surround you, destroy you, and go about their mess of an existence." Cerulean's voice sounded colder than it usually did. The dry, matter-of-fact tone he had irked me in a way I couldn't express. "If we destroy them first, then we live another day."

As he said that, we all looked out to see Gold happily punching his way through the crowd of Stagnant. All his hits made some sort of high-pitched *thunk*. He was nowhere near as strong as Merlot, but a hit with his gloves was enough to bounce some of the Stagnant into each other or on the ground. He made quick work of blazing through the Stagnant and started knocking bodies off Merlot.

With all of their supposed experience, they made the mistake of standing in one place for too long. It took seconds for the two of them to be surrounded, and we could no longer see them. I started to step forward. I didn't know what I was doing, but I wanted to be over there. I needed to see them. Quartz saw that I was walking by him. As he reached to pull me back, I stepped over from his grasp. I don't even remember having the thought to do that. I don't remember seeing him reach for me. I did remember looking back and seeing the shocked expression on his face and his body stretched out.

"Did you notice that it's cold in here?" Cerulean said. I looked at him, and I saw white air leaving his mouth. It had gotten even colder. "The Stagnant make the world cold and dull. These buildings were once full of light, color, and life. Then they came along. They bring everything down; they bring everything to a standstill. If they get their hands on you long enough, first, you feel cold. Then, you become sluggish and are barely able to pay attention. Your stare becomes vacant, and you lose the will to speak. As you grow colder, you'll feel like you're drowning, but you won't be able to do anything. Your mind knows that something is wrong—"

"But you won't don't care enough to do anything about it," I cut in, resting on my experience.

"Correct. Further, if they have their grip on you long enough, you die. Even if you get away, eventually, you'll feel the same symptoms. Then you'll walk off alone when you know no one is thinking about you, no one can see you, and you die. It's inescapable." I looked at Quartz, who was looking away, covering his mouth and near tears. I looked back at Cerulean and his face had not changed from his usual bored look, but I saw that his fists were clenched tightly. "If you want to survive, stay out of the way. We have a system. It works."

I opened my mouth to say something, and Cerulean's eyes got narrower. I was silenced.

In that moment, I realized I was looking up at him. "All you have to do is not annoy us with your ignorance."

I started to feel a chill inside of me. For a second, I shivered. It was like I was breathing ice. Quartz must have seen this. He gave Cerulean a scorn and gave me a hug. I didn't want his hug, but I desperately wanted his hug. I felt a bit warmer.

Out of the corner of my eye I saw blast after blast of Stagnant bodies fly in all directions. I could hear the sounds of grunts, groans, gloves, and high-pitched squawking of shoes. As Quartz started to let me go, Merlot charged through a wall of the Stagnant. As the crowd tried to collapse back in, Gold came charging through. It was he who was blasting the Stagnant in different directions. At some point, he had traded his gloves for a gold mallet that was at least three times his size. When they got through the crowd, I noticed that less than half of the Stagnant remained.

Gold smiled and knelt down on one knee and presented the mallet to Merlot with his head down. The angry, red-eyed man gave a wicked smirk and took the weapon. With three quick spins toward the Stagnant, Merlot released the mallet and obliterated most of the remaining mob on impact in a spinning sweep.

Then, on its own, the hammer's direction started to curve, and it took out another sizable group. As a cloud of black dust fell, only a few of the Stagnant bodies remained, but the hammer was curiously gone. Merlot launched himself forward and destroyed what was left of the horde by landing on them. The ground shook, and we could hear wood cracking. He stood, turned to us, and smiled. It was the first time I had seen him smile, and I could already tell it was forced, but he was trying to be genuine. Not a second later, he fell on his knees.

Freedom of Speech

***

Why are we so afraid to say what we mean? You won't hesitate to say you're happy. You want people to know when you succeed. We demonize the thoughts of sorrow and fear being spoken aloud. If it's because those emotions make us seem weak, then why are not all emotions weak? Emotion is a natural reaction, or it's not. A natural reaction is either acceptable or not. If there is a gray area, then you should be able to tell me why and what the criteria are for each category.

Why do people act like having emotion, a natural reaction, is such a problem? Are you pretending that you don't know what I'm talking about? I'm talking about how someone who can't physically get out of bed because they understand that life is the biggest joke ever, created by who knows and who cares, is looked at as weak. They're looked at as a problem, and if they talk about it, then you avoid them, like them telling you how they feel is a hex on you.

I'm talking about how if someone is upset because someone did something wrong to them, we tell that person to calm down. Basically, telling them to erase your anger for my sake. When someone is feeling afraid of something or so anxious they can't function properly, we make them feel like idiots. After all, it's all in their wild imagination, right?

I mean, who gets shot, stabbed, bombed, put in a war that they didn't ask for, loses a family member, does so poorly in school they can't get a job, spied on, taken advantage of, has an awkward moment, has a fatal disease, trampled by a crowd at the supermarket in this day in age? Who gets thought of as broken and worthless by strangers? Who gets judged? Even if those things happen you might be able to brush it off and keep going. As long as people don't make others think of their own problems and get sad when they don't want to, everything is fine. As long as you radiate a light that's warm and bright but not too bright, it's fine. Your inability to accept your reflection is quite sad. Full offense.

***

"Merlot?!" Gold called, rushing over to him.

Merlot's head dropped down. He was shaking. It seemed like he was fighting with his body to stay upward. He put his hand on Merlot's shoulder, then immediately took it back. He placed a hand over his mouth. Quartz ran over and slid down beside him and repeated the motion of placing his hand on his shoulder and pulling it away. Then he put it back. He placed his other hand on Merlot's cheek. The back of his hand ran up to his forehead and then below his chin. He slowly lifted his head up. Merlot's eyes were closed. Quartz threw both of his arms around Merlot and squeezed him tight. I heard faint sobbing.

Without really thinking about it, I started to walk forward. I felt someone catch my arm and yank me back. Looking back, I saw Cerulean lowering his hand, but he seemed too far away to have grabbed me. I looked at his face, or at least I tried to. He had his head down and eyes closed as well but Cerulean's were clearly forced closed. His mouth was a straight line, his body was stiff as it usually was, but now, he was perfectly still. I still felt a tight grip on my arm. It was starting to feel numb.

30

I tried to say something to him, but my voice seemed to have retired. I found the strength to try and wiggle my arm for two solid tugs. Cerulean walked past me, eyes still shut, head still down. My arm felt free. He stopped a few feet from me and turned so I saw his side. He held up a hand to me, and it shook. He turned and walked over to the others. I was stuck in place again. I think I should have been. I saw no reason for me to be there.

***

I, for one, wish things were better in this world. Everyone should be able to say whatever it is they want, in reason of course. That's not right. I mean, everyone should be able to express themselves in a way that doesn't hurt anyone. Right? Well, no, I suppose that's not it, either. Why is this so difficult to say? As long as no one...as long as you're...I think that we should be careful with what we say. What we say can greatly impact those around us.

As great as it would probably feel, you shift the negative feelings you're getting out into someone else. It may not be your intent, but that's the truth. If we watch what we express for now, eventually, we'll get more of an idea of what we can express with another person or group; when we're comfortable, we can express ourselves freely. Or we can talk to someone who is trained not to react to what we say. I know this sounds difficult and unideal but think of the negativity.

Think of the hurt you cast on someone else. Think about how insensitive you're being while you also want sensitivity. Think about the person you're talking to already having their world already crumble, and what you say making it worse. Think about how the last thing someone said before they took their own life being something you said because you said the first thing that came to your mind. Think of how much something someone said makes you feel angry or sad or helpless. Why would you want that for someone else? Think how happy you were when ignorance was still bliss. I just don't want to see anyone else in pain, ever. I'd rather be alone and in pain myself.

***

Cerulean walked over and leaned against the wall with his arms crossed beside Merlot. Quartz wouldn't let him go. Cerulean sighed sharply, and Quartz's head shot up to glare at him. Cerulean looked at him with a glare of his own. Gold, who the two had forgotten was in the room, stepped out between their lines of sight. Cerulean scoffed and looked off at nothing. Quartz rested his head on Merlot's shoulder. He gave him one long squeeze and a slow kiss on the cheek. Then he carefully laid him down flat on the ground. Quartz stood up, and Gold threw his arm around his shoulders and walked him out. The sobbing continued.

Cerulean's head rolled, and his glare shifted to Merlot. Merlot's expression was soft. Cerulean's grip on his own arms tightened. His body started to shake. His eyes tightly shut again. He shot off the wall and marched up to his comrade. The blue-eyed man nudged Merlot's side with his foot a few times. Merlot didn't stir or make a noise. Cerulean's face hardened. He geared his leg back and kicked Merlot's.

Other than the impact, Merlot still did not move. Cerulean scoffed and swiftly exited the room. Quartz came back without Gold or his tears. He took off his outer shirt and threw it over Merlot. Right after he did that, his hands kept moving back and forth between reaching for the shirt and grasping at his arms. Every time his hands got close to the shirt, he jerked them back. He went down on his knees and put his hand on Merlot's.

Gold appeared, standing over him and rubbing his shoulder. No one had realized that he was there, and just as soon as he came in, he left. Cerulean came back in with his hands on his head. Gold came back soon after, and they all just stood over Merlot. After a few minutes, Gold started to pace back and forth.

***

Honestly, say whatever it is you want. Just be ready for someone to say whatever it is that *they* want. It's a bitch of a two-way street when you forget that, but it must be done. We change what hurts us so often that people most similar to us don't even always agree on what is and isn't okay. Just take the chance, and if it's a bad shot, be ready to apologize and adapt, or offer a good reason and stand by your choice of words.

***

Cerulean knelt and picked up Quartz's shirt. He looked at Quartz with an annoyed expression, fanned one of his arms out, and let it slap on his hip, shaking his head. Quartz snatched the shirt and turned away from him, stifling a sob.

Gold stepped in between them again. His usual big smile had lost half its strength. Cerulean walked around Merlot and away from the group.

Whatever the three people standing were feeling, or were at least projecting, faded from their faces and demeanor. They were pulled back to the fallen copy and perched themselves around the body. None of them moved even an inch. They dejectedly stared at the body's face for a long time, though they weren't looking for anything. The atmosphere started to get colder and stale. It felt as if the air, almost as if it had free will of its own, was pushing the whole room down. The light in the room started to fade even with all the doors open.

The world seemed to be getting darker. The dull gray skies grew more and more saturated. Every second of motionlessness felt like a lifetime to the ones watching the body. Before anyone could notice, the sky finally went black. Everything around was black. In a way, it was peaceful. It didn't even feel like you were being brought down anymore, just there in the darkness. There was just nothing. *I was nothing.*

Someone screamed.

Someone cried.

Someone laughed.

Someone weakly told everyone to shut up.

"I'm not done yet, assholes."

***

Often, speaking is useless. Actions are not. You can hear someone's words and then take them to mean something different than they actually meant. You can ignore words. You can conveniently leave out words. People want to harp on people who don't speak much and then won't stop talking long enough for someone else to say anything. I get that you feel like you're talking to a wall at that point, but have you considered that maybe you're just afraid to be left alone with your own thoughts? Or maybe the reason that they aren't speaking is because they have the gull not to offend you. Or maybe they have the audacity to not want to make a fool of themselves.

Maybe they don't have loose lips like you, so they can't process their thoughts fast enough for your liking. I know this may come as a shock, but not everyone likes to talk just to talk. I know that sounds like a reach, but so is thinking someone is rude if they don't feel like speaking. A voice is a gift, and you should cherish it. Like the thing that you are really thinking about while waiting for your turn to speak. Some do that by speaking any time they want to, and some use it when they feel something needs to be said.

Honestly, say what's on your mind. It doesn't matter. People can be offended by a compliment, and an insult can be misinterpreted as a joke. Everyone seems to have selective hearing. Shift your tone, and suddenly, words don't matter. Lying is a norm no matter how many times you lie to yourself and say that it's not.

So, let your actions speak for you. If you're passionate about an issue, protest it, vote against it, try to change it. If you like someone, show it, don't give them a chance to not understand what you mean. Anyone can say that they have a friend, but are you there for them as much as they are for you? Are you making it a contest or billing them for favors? To show it in the actions that you perform speaks volumes. Talk is just fluffing the air.

***

The air in the room started to warm up and rise. No one made a sound. The skies outside started to lighten up a bit more. There still wasn't much light in the room, but it was enough to make out five very similar silhouettes. One silhouette was lying down but slowly rose to its feet by itself. One put something on and made itself more identical to the others. Four silhouettes stood before the fifth.

The group of four started to approach the lone one. The one on its own did not move. The four stood in a line before the one. There was no motion for some time. The sky lightened even more, but the details had not quite come back into the world. The four dark figures walked past the lone one, one of the four bumping into one as it passed. For the first time that I can remember, I felt myself smile. The small stream of light that cut into the windows and doorway burst into a flood.

The room was a gymnasium. Under mounds of black dust, red and blue lines decorated a glossy brownish-red floor. There were six basketball hoops coming from the ceiling surrounding the room. Beige and red bleachers that went from the floor to what looked like the heavens lined two opposite sides of the court. There were abandoned signs all around that said things like "fight" and "let's go Bears" in red glitter. There was a scoreboard in the back of the room where the group was dancing around that read a score of 105 for the Bears and 1 also for the Bears. The former had red lettering, and the latter blue. I heard someone call out to me from behind, and I walked out with the rest of the group.

The sun seemed to only be shining on the gym. I looked back and saw the building we were in. It was a light brown building with a dark blue roof, and the outside was surrounded by red gutters and big red flowerpots full of dirt. The sun was nowhere in sight. I turned back around and looked forward, and the light was getting weaker by the step.

***

Say what you want. It's what you're not saying that interests me the most.

***

We started walking down streets that I still couldn't fully see. Quartz looped his arm through mine. Gold started rubbing his eyes and flailing around, trying to tease Quartz about being dramatic, and Quartz only chuckled to himself. Cerulean and Merlot stuck close to each other and walked quietly, a little behind the three of us. Everyone seemed to know exactly where they were going in the dark. There was no talking about direction, just walking.

I stopped thinking about it. I stopped thinking about anything. Gold and Quartz's voices started to blend together.

I felt myself walking, but I couldn't get myself to stop or change course. I started to feel numb. It became harder to feel my body as a complete thing. It was like pieces were just flimsily glued to certain spots, and a motor was keeping everything moving. Every step became lighter. I felt like every part of me was becoming a mist. I felt my face freeze in a nothing expression.

I tried to think of what I was doing. I tried to yell out that I wasn't okay, and I needed someone's help to make me solid again. I couldn't tell if I was sinking, floating, or still just walking. Maybe I was starting to dissipate. Maybe that was okay. *Why wouldn't it be?* My thoughts started to become a soft, staticky buzz. My thoughts started to get quieter and quieter until I couldn't recognize them. What little I could see faded to black. Then Quartz squeezed my arm.

Feeling that pressure on my arm brought me back to feeling numb. It wasn't pleasant, but at least I was feeling *something*; I think that was better. I could hear Gold and Quartz as separate beings again. Quartz was telling Gold about how embarrassing the situation with the shirt was. Gold was trying to tell jokes about the shirt. Suddenly, we came to a stop. My legs kept moving until Quartz pulled me back. I heard a deep sigh come from four different mouths.

"What is it?" I asked.

"Well...nothing," Gold said. "Zilch, Zip, Zero, not a thing, not a hint of a thing, nada..."

"GOLD!" Merlot snapped. "We get it."

"Actually, I don't," I said.

"Shocker," Merlot said. I still couldn't see anything at all, but he said it in a way that made me sure that he was rolling his eyes.

"We've been walking around for a while and haven't seen anything, so why is that important now?"

"Stop asking good questions. We'll blow through the plot in two seconds."

"What?"

"There's supposed to be a path around this part of town that shows us the way to go easily to the other side," Cerulean said.

"A path?"

"It's like a road or street," Gold said. He let a beat pass. "Yes, I can feel that you rolled your eyes at that."

Religion

Is there a God? If there was, would I have a face like this? I guess I could change it, but then again, that's more science than miracle. Maybe they are one and the same. Would I have all this potential and live in a dump of a home in the Midwest? Eh, probably. I feel like it's a cop-out to say I don't know, but it feels fraudulent to say that I know for sure. Let's try this: I'll say what I know and trick myself into taking a stance.

Chocolate is amazing, mac and cheese alone is not a real meal, pizza and tacos are amazing foods but not a personality trait, God...pumpkins and tomatoes are fruit, I don't know that many facts. Mental health is unnecessarily stigmatized, God...humans should spend more time listening rather than talking because they usually end up arriving at the same conclusion via the same desire, hating another person because a physical difference or orientation is dumb, a group of ferrets is called a business, God...I don't know.

I mean, we've already talked about death, and that sort of ties in. What happens when it's all over? Who's right? Something I hate thinking about; people hate talking aboutit because if someone is right, that usually means that someone is wrong. Can't we all be right? Then again, I'm sure the ones who are right that nothing happens, we just see black, would probably be mad, jealous, and regretful when they find out that people are in Heaven experiencing their greatest fantasy.

Maybe the darkness is Heaven to minds like that. Peace without impact. Maybe your greatest fantasy is your Hell.

Reward without end or challenge. Should I do drugs? I feel like I would be the best at drugs. I do not endorse drugs for the record. Would a God let us think about these things? Did we get the answer and choose to ignore it or not document it properly? I don't know. If you feel that you do good for you.

I know something that I do know: a person's relationship with God or religion, in general, is completely their own, and not everyone who believes the same thing follows the same rules. Some people have complete faith that when they shower, they won't have to use the toilet after or that they'll swim cramp-free right after eating. I think I'm more concerned with how we treat each other on this plane of existence and how people are affected by my actions here. So, in a way, I'm my own God. Or maybe god? Either way I'm sure that's yet another complex that I have that I will ignore and randomly bring up at some point. Maybe when I'm happy, and I don't feel like I deserve it. Yeah, I'm sure I won't have anything else to do that day.

***

"Maybe if we all think really hard and say we believe..." Gold said.

"Don't," Merlot barked.

"It's not like we've seen the sun up and out in eons," Cerulean said.

"Yes, but we've also hadn't been making progress," Quartz said. "And that's been changing. Maybe we've strayed from the path we're supposed to be on."

"Life is more fun without a map," Gold said.

"And yet here we are with our thumbs up our asses," Merlot interjected.

"Actually, I think that's mine...OW!" Gold screeched.

"That was definitely your head. Let's just go."

"Where?" Cerulean asked in a way that wasn't really a question. "We are literally in empty black space."

"Wait none of you can see either?" I asked.

"Are you fucking new?" Merlot asked, with a great whine. "Yes, he is, I forgot, everyone shut up."

"When we spend a lot of time in one place, the environment gets darker," Cerulean said. "But if we were going the right way, a path of white lights would guide us straight to where we needed to be. This should be easy"

"Maybe we can't see the easy way..." I felt myself say. It was much easier to talk when I couldn't see them. "But if we go toward the right direction, even in an unconventional way we might find the easier path." I started to feel cold air slicing into me. "Or you know...at least, we'll...find our way there..." The cutting was getting stronger by the word.

"Eventually!" Quartz interjected.

"And it's not like we have anything better to do," Gold said. "I guess we could count and rank our insecurities again," Gold said. I chuckled to myself. The feeling of the coldness went away, but I still felt like there was less of me.

"Shut up and pick a direction," Merlot said.

"*Please* pick a direction," Quartz added.

"Let's just turn around and start that way." I couldn't see Gold, but his voice was directly in front of me. I felt a breeze whip at my left and an arm loop around my right.

"This way," Cerulean said behind me in a louder voice than usual. Quartz turned me around, changed his position, and started to lead me in the direction of Cerulean's voice.

"Hey, wait. You didn't correct him on the 'shut up' part," Gold said, but Quartz didn't respond, only giggled to himself. By the sound of the jovial whistling of one note and a rough groan behind me, I knew Gold and Merlot were following us. As we walked, every now and then, Gold would give a direction, and we'd go the opposite way. No one was talking this time.

***

There are too many questions associated with the topic of religion to ever accurately communicate with someone who doesn't share all, or at the absolute least majority, of your views. You can go back and forth for centuries and accomplish nothing more than a screaming match where both sides are saying, "You're wrong, and I'm the enlightened one." No one follows any set of rules perfectly, and when they do, they just change, so what's really the point? That's really what it all comes down to, right? What is the point?

What is the point of all the heartbreak? What is the point of fairness? What is the point of trying to be a good person? What is the point of not giving in to your urges? What's the point of willpower? What's the point of tradition? What's the point of bettering yourself? What's the point of procreating and being born? What's the point of life? None of us asked to be born.

None of us asked to live in a society.

None of us asked to be oppressed and hated for parts of our identity that we cannot and should not care to control.

None of us asked for our differences to make us unique.

None of us asked to go through the pain of watching the people in our lives die.

So, to cope with these trials and tribulations, we tell ourselves that there's a reward at the end of all this. There is someone who has seen us. They have seen what you have gone through. They have seen who you really are. They have seen you stick to the rules. They have seen your restraint. They know you are a good person and that you have done your best, and the long, repetitive cycle of nothingness, pain, happiness, trying, succeeding, and failing wasn't for nothing.

Surviving all leads to something. Some acknowledgment. Some peace of mind. Something good that you deserve. We're born to live selflessly so that we can die and finally be selfish? That doesn't sound right. Living selfishly means that you are punished when your life ends. Though, that is the most basic and generic version of belief. There are beliefs where there is no punishment. Everyone gets rewarded. There are beliefs that we just start over and keep starting over until we get life "right." Some believe that we just never truly go away; we exist in some form somewhere, and if the vessel we are in stops working or breaks, we find a new one.

When a child hears that one day they will die, it cuts them to the core. It leaves a nasty scar. Then we slap religion over that scar, and it stays there unless a person decides to rip it off and cast it away. Once you can see you can live without the bandage, you don't instantly feel free and gratified. You've just realized that you now don't have an answer when you are asked, "What's the point?"

Some people find comfort in that, for some, that itches their scar. They itch and itch until they have to scratch it. They scratch and tear open a wound. You bleed out with questions; you cry out in pain. It feels good to scratch, but the pain from this wound makes it feel wrong. *You* feel wrong. What is right? You can stop scratching, but that itch persists. You will trigger a bleed again. Maybe you'll find something else to cover the scar, and the itching will stop. You'll feel better. Maybe you'll never stop scratching, and the scar is infected with a poison that changes your mentality, and the scratching is replaced with distractions.

"I don't need to scratch at it. I can smoke."

"I don't need to scratch at it. I can have another drink."

"I don't need to scratch at it. I can take my discomfort out on him."

When you stop picking at it, a scab forms, and you lock the poison inside. Perchance, all of this was just a melodramatic circumlocutory that doesn't pertain to you and your indifference. A life beyond peradventure is a possibility we often think unachievable. Or maybe we are just over thinking the concept of don't be a dick to people because it doesn't feel good and won't make your life less of a shit show.

***

Walking in the dark is a weird experience. It's troubling when everything blends together, and you start to float away, but this was uncomfortably comfortable. Every step was like walking in a pool. Half floating, half falling, pushing through something that's not really resisting you and isn't even holding form. We stepped carefully but surely. Even I realized that stopping to reassess things meant that another wave of Stagnant would come. I felt myself closing the loop tighter on Quartz's arm, and I felt his hand rest on my arm. Thankfully, it didn't take long for us to come across something.

We rounded a corner, and in front of us, there were rays of golden light shining down behind the silhouette of a building. There was enough light to see there were more houses on one side and an empty open space on the other. We were coming up on the side that had nothing. I felt Quartz pulling me, and we all started running. I could hear Gold laughing behind me. We were in a full sprint going toward this house.

We didn't stop to look at the front, but we did go around to the backside, where the light was shining down. We passed by a tall and luscious pear tree that had pink petals and sweet smells being carried over to us by the wind. We were walking on dull grass. There was an extremely tall tree that I could not see the top of no matter how much I cocked my head back. It was much taller than the one-story house we were behind, maybe five times over. There was a huge nest of branches surrounded by logs.

Next to that was a big square of gray concrete blocks holding an overflowing bush of tall grass with white, violet, and green flowers. Next to it was a small concrete square column with two big rough concrete tabs on either side. The further we walked into this area, the more it sloped up. There was a wall of thick, tall, red, and green stalks with broad leaves. It was like a bamboo forest in a field.

To the side of all this was a wall of overhanging bushes with all kinds of leaves and vines with red and dark-colored berries. Above that were trees with low-hanging branches with yellowish green leaves and very small, light green apples. All this was interweaving with all this dark green foliage. Looking closely, in all of this was a warped and rusted metal fence. Next to that was the house I'm surprised we were all ignoring. It's not because it was unremarkable, though it was. It's that we were in a new place and were ignoring this building.

It was all white with a dirty gray concrete bottom layer. There was a long window on the right side with brownish-orange curtains blocking the view inside. On the left side, the was a regular window that had dingey white curtains and thick, black bars on the outside that looked like lace. In the middle, there were two gray steps leading up to a glass door that had a black curtain covering it from the inside and longer, thick, black bars across the outside.

The light seemed to cut off past the other side of the pear tree, and you could no longer see beyond it. Between the pear tree and the concrete column in the corner was a massive green bush full of white roses with pinkish-purple and red rings. There were small, low-to-the-ground blue and violet flowers that came up from the ground in random places in small clusters. I took in a deep breath and smelled the sweet air with a delightful sting of a grassy undertone.

I let the air go out of my mouth and became aware of the warmth from the light and the perfectly cool air rolling over me. I breathed in and out again, and I felt myself standing up straighter with no effort when the air was gone. I took another breath in, and I could hear birds start to sing and the rustling of thousands of leaves. I breathed out, then in again, and warm tears fell from my eyes. I let the breath go and smiled. I felt good. I felt safe.

I went to the wall of red and green stalks. The ones at the front were taller than me. I pushed my way inside, and the world got quieter, and the stocks got bigger and more spaced out with bigger leaves. The way that the light peaked in between the small gaps in the leaves was mesmerizing. I sat down on the sloping dirt floor and let the swaying stalks and rustling leaves hypnotize me. I looked forward through the leaves to see Merlot climbing the tree. He went so high up I couldn't see him anymore.

Quartz sat on one of the concrete tabs, jetting out from the column in front of me. He waved at me and turned the top of his body toward the flowers. He smiled sweetly and let out a breath of air as he leaned back on the column. I couldn't see Gold and Cerulean, so I started to crawl over toward the wall of berries and vines. The forest of stalks didn't stretch out far enough to make it halfway through the yard, but I moved far enough to see the others.

***

We can't be alone in the universe, can we? Humans on Earth can't be all there is in terms of sentience. Living and dying can't be it for us, right? To just come in one day and then not exist another; that doesn't make any sense. To be bogged down by crushing dark thoughts for so long and, at the end of it, just nothing? Thinking nothing, doing nothing. The only relief the most messed up of us get is just to die, and even then, we can't really enjoy it. We just don't do anything?

So, there are people who will never know what it means to live? Do any of us? They say not to rush into death, but it seems like you run the gambit on whether it's all worth it or not. Life can be pleasant, and the transition into death can be troublesome, but when the length of the transition is greater than that of the life you live, is the trouble worth it? Is that what religion or believing is? A reason why it's worth it? We can't be alone. If we were, wouldn't people just rush to die? But dying early is bad.

But then again, if we aren't alone, wouldn't people rush to die then, too? I suppose there is comfort in knowing that no one truly knows because every person has a different idea, and that, too, is also something so terrifying to me. But then again, there is something very comforting that there are people who feel this way. That's sad, and a bit selfish, and messed up, but that's all I got. Maybe that's just what faith is: a community of scared, confused people exploring one theory to keep them running through the gambit. Whether you are as confused as people like me or as confident as all get out, we all just pick a theory and run the gambit. That, for lack of a better idiom, is something I can live with.

***

Gold was pulling branches down, which made most of the wall sink in. He pulled the branch so far down he was able to sit on the ground. He gave the branch its freedom, and it shot back up high into the air and fell back into place. This threw many of the small green apples into the air. Gold caught every one of them, all seven of them, and then immediately started to try and juggle them. Quartz quietly clapped and cheered for his efforts. I think this made Gold try harder to impress Quartz more than anything.

I finally noticed Cerulean sitting on a log. He looked up at the clouds above. He had a stick in his hand and was dragging it all about in the dirt by the branch pile. Other than his hand, he didn't move. He just sat there, looking up. I wondered if he was focused on something I couldn't understand. *I'm always the one who doesn't know anything.* I think I lost focus for a second and let my hands slip. I caught myself before falling.

I looked around and tried sticking my face out in different spots, but I could not see Merlot. I sat down again. I took three deep breaths. I wondered how high Merlot climbed. *I could never get more than a foot off the ground. I couldn't do anything.* I must have lost focus again. I was lying in the dirt, and I don't remember getting down on the ground. I just stayed there. I noticed the light wasn't as strong anymore. There were fewer birds chirping. The air was cooler but not cold.

From my angle, I could see that Gold was finally able to juggle all the apples. *Performing for no one.* I inhaled sharply, and the air came out roughly. I could see that Quartz heard that and was getting up. I knew he was going to come in, and I didn't want that. This was my forest. I crawled out and Quartz helped me to my feet. He took out his red cloth and tried dusting me off.

Why did he care? Was I that much of an embarrassment?

I abruptly walked away and sat on the slab on the opposite side of the column. It was cool to the touch, and I could feel the texture of the slab grinding on my jeans. I changed my position so that I was sitting on my bent left leg. I could see into the column and was shocked to see it was hollow. I looked into it and saw black coals that were half ash, leaves that were both dead and alive and carrots that were half eaten clearly by a small mouth.

The tree in front of me that Merlot had climbed had three big, connected segments. It had a crevice that looked like a foothold. I took a deep breath and sprang from my seat. I don't know where I got the confidence to do it, but I started to climb. I stomped in the foothold, and I was two feet off the ground. I slammed on the big segment of the tree in front of me. I put one foot up and stepped up while I pulled myself up using the bark. I used the opposite foot and did the same thing. I repeated this motion until I was at the same level as the roof of the house.

There was a branch that was thick and long, jetting out toward the house. I looked down and gave myself a fright. I climbed upward to where I somehow convinced myself was safety. I climbed on and sat down on the branch. I wrapped my legs around it at first. Once I got my balance, I swung one leg up and let it rest on the branch. I still could not see Merlot.

***

I pray a lot. I'm not sure who's listening or if anyone is listening, but I pray. I don't even know what I would do with the information if I knew for sure either way. I can imagine being pissed that I wasted so much time to find out nothing matters. Then relieved that I had no one to impress with my life. I'd be pissed that someone was up there just watching everything and letting me go through so much. Then maybe relieved that I have someone other than myself to talk to. I think that's why I pray. It's more than a hope. It's more than a wish. I don't pray for myself that much; I don't deserve it, and I don't think anything would happen.

I don't always think that anything that happens for the people I pray for is because of me. It's a comfort almost. I'm powerless, and I hope that someone or something is willing to help. It's selfish more than selfless. I could do more; I could always do more. I just sit there and hope-pray. At least I can acknowledge that it doesn't work.

If prayers work, mine probably don't. I'm probably going to hell. I'm no angel because I'm depressed. The things a person may have to do to keep going can be both horrendous and exhausting. So many people that I hurt and stepped on, stepped over, in the name of keeping going. So many violations of friendships. So many stupid friendship tests that my idiotic brain designs for everyone to fail. So many pointless fights I start because I can't stand the idea of someone even tolerating this trash. I seek information that I'm not supposed to know and use it against myself.

I took advantage of so much trust so that someone could tell me every private thought they have about me and flip it. I tortured myself with not knowing. I'll come up with a million reasons why you must secretly hate me, and this is all just a trap. Someone as amazing and accomplished as you could not possibly have an iota of care for me. Once I know, I torture myself for knowing. How dare I force that out of you, knowing full well that you were genuinely here for the friendship, and I shouldn't have a problem. I don't know what trust is, and I refuse to find out, apparently.

Fight after fight. Sabotage after sabotage. It's always their fault to me. I lie to myself and convince myself that's the truth. I forge a blade made of hopes, dreams, and insecurities set on a hilt of despair, sharpen it with a dull silver tongue, and go for the jugular after an ambush. I make sure that you're okay before I leave you, or more likely, you leave *me* in my misery. Little do you know I dunked that blade in the poison pool of my misery, and it will stay with you even if the scar goes away. I will make your world a little darker. I make my own *a lot* darker.

When I see you around and hear of your accomplishments, I say a prayer. I pray that my darkness and your darkness get together and leave you and find their way back to me. I can't forget you, but please forget me. I bring despair and tragedy everywhere I go. I'm either a broken creation of God who couldn't have known what plague was being unleashed or just another broken asshole. Both perhaps.

I know life is filled with irony and makes us all feel stupid, so why would an afterlife be different. Hell, for me, is myself with other people. After everything I do just to keep going until the natural end, I may just end up doing it all again. *That's* what I deserve.

***

I did see empty nests, a lot of leaves that were turning yellow and red. I looked down and saw Quartz watching me and

Gold trying to get Quartz's attention by throwing the fruit he had been juggling. Except for his hand, Cerulean still did not move. I was too far up to see what he had been doing. The air smelled different up in the tree. The pear smell was stronger but was overshadowed by wood. I didn't get much air due to the surrounding leaves, but they made up for it with the excited shaking they made. I glanced down in time to see Gold accidentally hit Cerulean with an apple. The blue-eyed boy did not react.

Gold apologized and Quartz looked at the spot where the apple struck him. I caught myself laughing. I stopped myself and stared at Cerulean. He didn't react. No one reacted. I smiled and laughed a little. Then I laughed at Cerulean being hit with the apple again. I didn't stop myself. I went with it. I laughed harder, then laughed at myself for laughing so hard. Then I laughed at the apple again. I laughed because I could. I laughed so hard tears fell. I laughed at the tears. I started coughing because it became hard to breathe. I didn't want to breathe. I wanted to laugh. I laughed and laughed.

I laughed at how much of a joke I was.

I stopped paying attention and started falling. I stopped laughing.

I closed my eyes and mouth as tight as I could, and my whole body tensed. I stopped breathing. I was ready for the fall. Seconds passed, but I could not feel the ground. I felt like my body was weightless. I could feel the air caress my entire body. I did not move. It felt like I couldn't even if I wanted to. I sat in suspension for a while and finally caught my breath.

Then, I felt myself move. My eyes popped open in shock. I looked down, and I was now standing on the branch. Quartz had his hands over his mouth, Gold had his hands over his eyes but was still peaking. What surprised me the most was that Cerulean had moved. He had his hand stretched out with his palm toward me. His blue eyes cut through me again, but I had to keep telling myself that I couldn't dwell on that at the moment. I remembered that I almost fell out of the tree. I looked back behind me and saw that I had a steadfast grip on the tree, and I was breathing heavily. I don't know many things—*I'm sure that was clear*—but I know I didn't do that.

Before Quartz could come up or tell me to do anything, I slowly started to climb down. Once I got down on the ground, I looked at Cerulean, and he paid me no mind. He just looked up at the sky, which was now getting dark. This was a new type of dark that I hadn't experienced. There was light, just less of it. Not golden, but silvery. *I couldn't believe I barely remember the moon.* The area started to get quiet.

All I had accomplished so far was being useless and falling out of a tree. *How can I waste the day away like that? I knew that something was coming. Why can't I just focus? Why am I even trying? I'm going to fail. I am a failure.* I finally could see what Cerulean was doing in the dirt. He drew a series of lines going in every direction. There were stars at certain points that looked like he was creating a trail.

At the base of it, he wrote: "DON'T GO BACK IN THERE EVER AGAIN" in squiggly and deep lines and circled a lot. I didn't understand what he meant by this. I did get that something was disturbing him. I saw that he wrote his name over and over again and the word "breathe." I tried to imagine what all this meant. *I don't know anything.* I couldn't decipher it. *Because I'm an idiot.* Maybe his name was important. *He was important enough to get a name.* Maybe it meant nothing. *Like m—*

I felt two hands on my shoulders. It was Quartz who was looking straight at me. His face was unusually serious. It was unnerving. He smiled, and I felt myself breathe out and relax my shoulders. Quartz lowered his arms. *Good, I didn't deserve his care.* He put them back up and gave me a squeeze. I tried to smile for him. The moon was now out. It was dark everywhere but light enough to still see the surroundings, from the wall of fruit to the pear tree and roses. The day was over. *Wasted*

"Where did the colors go?" I asked no one in particular. I heard a crack in my words. My eyes started to sting.

"They're still here," Quartz said in a hushed tone with a hand on my shoulder. "It's just dark. They'll be there when the light comes back out."

"Will it ever come back?"

"It did. So many times. We're beating this."

"You say that, but..."

"Hey, look at me," Quartz uttered a little more firmly. I looked into his eyes. For the first time, I noticed Quartz had very dark circles and drooping bags under his eyes. I couldn't really see the pink anymore. "We're going to get you to a safe place. This place will be colorful and not broken." *Broken.* "Everyone will come back to stay, so no one will ever be alone." *Alone.* "This is okay because we will be okay. We *are* okay." *None of this is okay.*

"*I'm* not okay," I said. I bit my tongue. I shocked myself because I didn't mean to say that out loud. I felt like profusely apologizing. I grabbed myself and backed away wishing I would vanish.

"Stagnant!" I heard a rough-sounding doppelganger shout. One of us jumped down from the tree. "We need to move our asses now!" he said. I found it so comforting that Merlot was here, it barely registered in my mind what he had just said.

***

Religion is the expression of your beliefs and worship over something or someone. That's pretty much it. There are people who follow religion in a strict or literal way and there are people who follow religion in a loose way. There are people who do bad things in the name of religion, and there are those who use religion as a pillar to why they do good things. There are some people with religions that may be perceived as odd to someone who believes in something else. You can choose not to belong to religion, and if someone is forcing you to, that is wrong; it's a choice. Religion is just religion.

Am I religious? I believe that having a network of people who believe the same thing and support their community is a tremendous thing. Everyone should want something like that. I wish I had something like that. I think it's wonderful that people have something that makes them feel accepted and part of something. I like that although there is exclusion, there is another community that loves and accepts twice as hard. Although there is bad, there are communities that do twice as much good. Do you need to be in a religion to experience all the good or even bad things? No. We're just humans trying to live. Do I believe in someone out there? Does it matter? Let's just live our lives.

***

"Cerulean, where do we go?" Quartz asked.

"They're already here," Cerulean said, looking toward the wall of fruit and foliage. We all looked over. The air had gone fowl and was so strong it stung my tongue and made me gag. The wall shifted, and we could hear loud moaning. They were coming through slowly, and there were a lot of them. I couldn't even see the end of them. Quartz grabbed Cerulean and me by the hand and took us to the other side of the yard.

We stopped short of leaving the scene. There was nothing beyond the rose bush. Not just an empty field, not just darkness, but nothing. A pitch-black void. Quartz took a step on that side and almost fell into the nothing before Cerulean pulled him back. I couldn't tell what was lucky: him getting pulled back or almost falling in. We looked over. The pear tree had fallen and was blocking our way to the front.

We turned around and saw Gold and Merlot backing up to us. We looked past them and saw that the Stagnant had filled the yard. There were leagues more Stagnant here than back at the gym. It hurt to breathe. The air was no longer sweet, but sour and musty. I saw sporadic puffs of white air come from my mouth. I held myself to shield my skin from the cold air attacking me. Quartz wrapped himself around me. It didn't do much, but it helped. We were surrounded.

"C-Ceru-ru-lean?" Quartz cried out in a strained whine. His face winced as he squeezed me tighter. Cerulean didn't answer him, he just stood there, shaking. I didn't think that was a feature he possessed. He bawled his fists up tight and slammed them against his legs.

"There's far too many," Cerulean he finally said. He growled and looked down. Merlot let out a fierce yell and clapped his hands together. A strong boom and an equally strong gust of wind knocked a lot of the Stagnant away in front of us, but there were too many to matter.

"I'm not…" Merlot trailed off. He was bent over and had a strong grip on his thighs. He was shivering hard. I tried to break from Quartz to help him, but he wouldn't let me go. Quartz was shivering so hard I wasn't sure he *could* let go. "I-I'm not…"

"Strong enough, I know," Cerulean said. "We can get in an arrow formation and breakthrough. We'll lose one of us…"

"Ab-solutely-ly not!" Quartz snapped.

"Be rational. It's better that *some* of us survive and get away from here. Staying a whole group wasn't bound to last. You've seen what happened to all the others."

"And I-I wo-o-on't go through that again!" A huge cloud of white air blasted out.

"It's inevitable," Cerulean said. I felt like I was cracking on the inside hearing that. I had no idea what they were talking about, and I wasn't being addressed, but that made me feel horrible. "We can't save everyone. We shouldn't have to. We don't even deserve to be alive—"

"I hate to interrupt your sure-to-be-tear-jerking soliloquy…" Gold said in an amplified voice. We looked ahead to the clearing Merlot made to see Gold in a shiny gold suit with a large dark blue and gold bowtie. He had matching gold running shoes. He was holding a microphone that was all gold with raised stars. "But God knows the audience is so sick of those by now."

"N-Not this again," Merlot groaned.

"Would you rather stop existing?" Gold asked.

"Yes!"

"Get on with it," Cerulean said as he and the rest of us ran over to Gold as the Stagnant closed in on us. I opened my mouth to say something, and Cerulean whirled his head around and down at me. "Quiet," he said. I felt myself shaking more. I stopped caring if the Stagnant got to me, but Quartz kept pulling me along.

"That Cerulean..." Gold continued. "Always the warm and snuggly type. I once saw him tell a crying child who had just lost a favorite toy that we're all going to die someday. So, the kid started crying harder. I asked him, 'Why'd you do that?' He said, 'Simple.'" Gold sighed, standing up straighter and imitating Cerulean's manner of speaking. "If the toddler is so irreverently irrational and disconsolate over an archaic plaything, then either a vexatious situation would illuminate essential perspective that would either breed cessation of the infernal clamoring or provide a more just and favorable rationale for the sobbing."

"The length of that sentence was atrocious," Cerulean said.

"But you don't deny the content," Gold said quickly. The Stagnant stopped moving, and there was a long, high-pitched, inconsistent moaning. "So then Merlot tried to get the kid to stop. He marches up to the kid." He raised his shoulders up and stomped around. He groaned and patched on an exaggerated frown. "He said, 'Hey kid,'" Gold said in a gruff voice. "'Shut up. Shut up, child.' Seriously, he said, 'child,'" Gold said normally. The moaning got higher, louder and started and stopped abruptly. "Of course, the kid isn't stopping. One guy just told him he was going to die, another that looked almost exactly like him tells him to shut up." The moaning started to get a lot less eerie. It almost sounded bouncy. "So, to round off this cacophony of dumb... Cacophony? What am I a Blue? So, to round it out, here comes Quartzy."

He relaxed his posture, tilted his head, and smiled very broadly. "He said 'oh sweetie' in that candy-coated voice he does." It seemed like it was much easier for him to imitate Quartz. "He said, 'Sweetness, it's okay. The mean boys are just being silly. It's okay to have feelings. They are the most magical, lovely, fantastic things around! Come here. Express your feelings to *me*! And he got on his knees and hugged the kid, holding him way too tight. The kid finally stops crying, and now he's just confused and annoyed. The kid looked at him like this..."

Gold crouched down and looked up, annoyed at an imaginary Quartz. The Stagnant started to laugh. Slowly, the laugh became less and less uniform, and you could hear multiple laughs from different bodies. The dark mass bounced up and down. There were spots where it started to crumble into dust. "I swear that kid stood up, aged like ten years, and walked away. He was *done* with us. He went to get a job and 401k; he could not handle us children anymore. He did say one thing as he was leaving, though. He turned back and said, 'Figure out what you believe in, and maybe your words would have more substance.'" He paused and let soft laughter die out. "Translation: get your life together, or you'll be a broke comedian being held captive by the audience." The Stagnant laughed harder.

"We should go," Cerulean said.

"Cerulean folks, in such a hurry to run out and tell someone they're wrong or dumb."

"Let's go!" Cerulean beckoned. Gold's torso was pulled forward, and he stumbled into a run. Quartz pulled me out, and Merlot followed.

"Intermission!" Gold called as we fled the scene from the laughing Stagnant.

We ran out of the broken ring of Stagnant and into the front. We looked over, and the was still a void on one side. We started to run the other way, but we saw a new Stagnant cloud pouring in. We heard a loud, groaning noise. It didn't sound sad. It sounded angry. I felt my core vibrating. I started bending over. My knees were so weak I fell and took Quartz down with me.

"In the house," Quartz said.

"NO," Cerulean and Merlot yelled.

"We go in or die," Quartz said in an uncharacteristically flatter pitch and stern tone.

"Dying doesn't sound so bad," Gold said.

"Come on!" Quartz said, rising and picking me up. He waved the other three toward the door. I was worried about what we were going to experience in the house. *Maybe Gold was right?* It was a small one-story, mostly red house with the bottom quarter before the faded dark red concrete foundation painted white. It had one long window in three sections, with more black bars in front of all the windows.

Even without the bars, you couldn't see inside because it had dirty yellow and brown curtains covering the windows inside. There was a straight concrete slab walkway leading to three short steps to a porch. It had heavily chipped green paint around the edges. There were bent and rusted white painted metal banisters that had decorative curves going up to a white with a red bottom stripe painted metal awing. There was a thin metal white door with two dark orange glass panels on either side of a black pane of glass. Quartz opened that, and there was a black door with a badly scratched knob that may have, at one point, been gold. Quartz hesitated to touch the door. Gold patted his back and moved past him to open the door.

Gold approached the door and turned the knob. There was a barrage of sounds coming from the inside. It just sounded like angry yelling from multiple people, but for once, none of them sounded like us. It wasn't as comforting as I thought it would be. Just thinking about that made me shrink into myself. The air was rich with something moldy on top of stale smoke. My throat stung like the air was digging in claws, refusing to go into my lungs. I coughed and gagged while Quartz patted my back.

We moved briskly through a room full of smoke and mismatched, very worn furniture. I couldn't see where we were going, and I was just pulled in a direction. I heard what sounded like curtains opening. We all plowed forward, and then I heard curtains closing. I felt Quartz dropping down, and I dropped down with him. I scuttled away a bit to give us both more space.

This place that we were in had a window that was partially covered in something with a lot of holes. I could see the sky was still pretty dark, and it hadn't gotten any brighter. I felt the cold and uneven wooden floor beneath me. There were deep, wide grooves on the floor. They were so deep that I could stick my finger down to the first joint. There were craters on the floor as well. These felt smoother and shallower than the grooves, but that didn't excuse their presence to me.

I heard someone messing with something in front of me and then electric crackling. With a click, there was light in the room. Not enough to see everything, but I could see Quartz next to me, Gold lying on his side next to him, Cerulean sitting down across from me, and Merlot against a wall. The walls were riddled with holes both deep and wide and shallow and small. Merlot kept shifting his weight and grumbling to himself, upset with the little space he had. The light source was a television projecting a bright static screen. It was a small gray box with shallow white scratches. I noticed a few scratches that looked like crude drawings of balloons.

The room we were in was small, and I saw a lot of outlines of things surrounding us. What little I could make out were boxes full of random things like more boxes, old toys, and electrical cords. The voices we heard when we came in didn't get that much quieter, but the air was at least a bit more breathable, though now the moldy stench was stronger.

I waited for someone to say something.

Mental Health

***

Why do I bother to care for anyone when no one cares for me? No one acknowledges my sacrifices or efforts. What's the point? No one cares about me. I can't do anything to make them care. Why do I care? Why do I love them? Do I love them? What is wrong with me? I don't belong in this world. It would be better for everyone if I just vanished.

***

"We can't stay here too long," Cerulean said.

"No shit," Merlot said. His energy and voice were low. He banged his head softly against the wall.

"What do we do?" Quartz asked, his voice low, too.

"We head back to base," Cerulean said. "We made more progress than we could hope for. We know the invasion is just too much for us to handle now. We can't keep running from the Stagnant. They'll take us all down." He paused and pondered for a moment. "We need to go before we get to the point where we can't."

"So, we go back, disappoint Inverno, and what?" Gold asked. His voice being flat and low made me shutter.

"I don't know," Cerulean said. Everyone's eyes darted in his direction.

"What do you mean you don't know?" Merlot asked.

"I don't know," Cerulean repeated, his eyes fixed on the floor.

"Bullshit," Merlot said, leaning over to him to study his face.

"If you know that, why even ask?"

"If you know it's shit, then why say it?" Gold remarked.

"Why is it up to me all the time to say what's on all our minds?" Cerulean said, his voice becoming more strained.

"That's not the point!" Merlot exclaimed, slamming his back and head to the wall.

"Because you want to put it all on me!" Cerulean said, exclaiming louder and looking him in his eyes. "Every single thing is on me. Why? Because I actually think about things? Because I actually look at things like they're meant to be looked at? Because I'm honest? I don't go through life with Quartz-colored glasses."

"Fuck you too," Quartz grumbled, my heart sank. I wrapped my arms around myself and scooted back away further from them. I shuffled between covering my ears and holding myself. In that moment, I didn't want to be there, but it also felt like I wasn't. "Sorry if I'm more concerned with trying to keep us moving forward than making us all want to off ourselves."

"Maybe we *should* off ourselves," Gold said.

"Gold...?"

"No. The chances of us making our way back to Inverno aren't even slim. They're nonexistent. It's not like they care either way."

"You can't say that!"

"Why not? They're not going to smite me. They'd have to be *around* to tell me if that offended them. They'd have to be around to tell me if they even felt *anything* for me...for *us*...for anything at all. They're supposed to be the best of us. What does it say when the best of us won't even come around to see if their own creations aren't falling apart? They probably don't even care about the colors being gone. They didn't care when the Stagnant got the others."

"*Gold!*" Quartz said.

"You're right. We already did the religion monologues. Why rehash this?" He started drawing circles on the floor with his fingers. As I looked closer, I could see he was already surrounded by circular grooves on the floor.

***

Why do I feel the need to make everyone smile and laugh and get so shocked when I'm equated to a joke? Why can't I smile for real? What's the point? No one cares about me! I can't do anything to make them care. Why do I care? Why do I hate them? Do I hate them? What is wrong with me? I don't belong in this world. It would be better for everyone if I just vanished.

***

"Perhaps they thought we could be self-sustaining," Cerulean said.

"Then they're an idiot."

"I said that same thing when you were created," Merlot said. The group snickered.

"Fuck off."

"I said the same thing when Merlot was created," Cerulean said. The group laughed a little harder.

"At least when they got here, we knew what they were," Quartz said. "It took ages to realize your thing wasn't that you are just a jerk."

"Wait, that's not his thing?" Merlot quipped. He, Cerulean, and Quartz laughed loudly. Gold just looked at the wall behind the television. The white wall suddenly gained splashes of yellow paint.

"Thanks, Gold," Quartz said, still chuckling.

"It's not like I did anything."

"You did *your* thing."

"You guys did 'my thing.' I'm not even good at it. I can sit for hours and not even make myself laugh. I can't come up with a single thing. I only make jokes when I'm nervous."

"You're always cracking jokes."

"Yup...You know what my favorite philosopher and personal hero says, 'Don't take life too seriously. You'll never get out of it alive.'"

"Elbert Hubbard?" Cerulean asked with a confused expression.

"Bugs Bunny." The blue-eyed copy gave a silent confirmation.

"At least you make people smile," Merlot said. He paused and sighed. "I don't want to be angry all the time. I just...am. Nothing in this damn world is fair. No one makes an effort to just sit and listen."

"We're listening," Quartz said, reaching out for him.

"We're each other! We have to listen." Quartz sat back and sighed.

"Trust me, no, we don't," Cerulean said. "Sometimes the voices are just so loud. You can't really hear the ones telling us that this is all worth it."

"Do you really think there is one out there at this point?"

"I don't know."

"Then you're as useless as I am," Gold said. "Welcome to the club."

"See what I mean?" Merlot said. "First, we make Merlot look like an idiot, then we focus on someone else."

"What do you want from us?" Quartz asked.

"How about some recognition! I practically carried your fat asses the entire time up to this point!"

"Right, because I don't fight, too," Gold said, rolling on his back and putting his hands on his stomach.

"Not as hard as me, clearly," Merlot said, grabbing his arm.

"Because I don't get reckless? Fine, I'll take that."

"You hide behind me as much as Quartz."

"Oh, do get off your high horse!" Quartz said. His voice started to deepen, and he put two fists on his hips. The cheer and the vigor were fading out. "You act like this spoiled brat all the time. 'Look at me! I'm so big and strong! Look at me!'" he said, his voice sounding more and more like Merlot's. "No one pays attention to me! I'll just throw another tantrum! I'll just walk around telling everyone to shut up and distance myself from everyone while staying by them the whole time. Why? Because they're my only friends, but since I can't find a place to channel my anger, I'll take it out on them. I'll give them a reason to eventually reject me, then blame them for changing on me. It's almost like I'm smart enough to predict they would do that but don't have the stability or maturity, but I can't see past my childish needs and stop it from happening.'"

"I'm *childish*?" Merlot asked, his voice calm and slow. "Childish for thinking that you all wouldn't accept me? You guys don't even accept yourself. Especially you and Gold. Playing the fool because you're afraid to show your actual selves." The more he spoke, the more he sounded like Quartz. His grip was tightening on his arm. "You hide behind people and only pipe up when you need to tell them they are wrong. You need to tell them that you are there to be the savior and make it all better, but you need the most saving. You're more fragile than the lightest glass cannon.

"The saddest part is that, of course, we know you can do it. We believe in you. You're the only one who doesn't. Trying to hide that you have the brains to lead the team because you're unsure you can do it. Afraid to finish a battle alone because you doubt yourself, and you know that can be your end. You hide behind bad jokes because you think that it hides yourself. You think it will make people forget your faults if they just think you're the funny one. That if they laugh at what you say, they won't laugh at you. But the truth is your actions are just laughable.'" Quartz looked up at the wall with the TV, and pink splashes of paint started to appear alongside the yellow.

"Laughable?" Cerulean said. He looked to the ceiling with a scrunched-up face and moved his head back and forth. He seemed to be pondering something amusing as he held a hand over his mouth to stifle a chuckle. "Sure. I guess."

"Don't fan the flames," Quartz warned. His face was serious, but very tired. His brow was furrowed, his voice deep, he wagged a finger at Cerulean, but his body hunched over. His eyes were fluttering like they wanted to shut, his head was lower than it needed to be, so he wasn't fully looking Cerulean in the eye.

"Or what? You'll do nothing? You'll nag me? What will the great Quartz do?

"Why should I do anything anymore? One day, you all will just kill each other, and I'll finally get some peace and quiet. You guys squawk so much that I don't know if I'm traveling with people or seagulls. You guys make more noise than a herd of hyenas getting tortured. Even when you are just running, you sound like a pack of chew toys getting chewed on by an enthusiastic dog." Although clearly angered, he almost sounded happy. His voice sounded like Gold's. "I guess not you, 'Ru. You sound like a walrus doing an impression of an aristocrat. No, no, like Tweety Bird trying to sound like an old lady from *Downton Abbey*. Do you know what you really sound like? You sound like a loser. A loser who must distance himself from the world because you're so far up your own big, fat ass that you honestly believe that you're better than the rest of us. You think that because you learned a few facts, that genuinely makes you smarter?"

Quartz began to laugh and sway his body. "You think we're the savages for expressing ourselves in perhaps a less controlled manner...but keep in mind that you, my friend, believe anything a *book* tells you. Anything you learn in the street is a magical anomaly that just seems to pop up for no good reason. Because with you, a fact is one lonely thing that has no real companion or opposition. You are the biggest joke of all." Merlot looked at the wall, and red splashes appeared with the other colors. The wall almost had no white left.

Cerulean started to laugh. Not a quick, dry chuckle like he usually did, but a deep, hearty laugh. It filled the room. It filled every person in the room. Everyone started to squirm, shudder, and shrink into themselves. They couldn't look at each other, so they all stared at different walls. Tears started to fall from Cerulean's eyes. Quartz clutched his arm. Then, replaying his own words, he dropped his arm and clenched his fists. He tried to harden his facial expression, but he looked quite uncomfortable. His whole body relaxed into a sigh and a whimper.

***

Who am I performing my intelligence for? I don't even appreciate my knowledge. I hate it. The more I know, the more I know I don't know, and the more I know I'll never learn everything. Why can't I let it go? What's the point? No one cares about me. I can't do anything to make them care. Why do I care? Why do I tolerate them? Do I tolerate them? What is wrong with me? I don't belong in this world. It would be better for everyone if I just vanished.

***

"Shut the fuck up, you miserable waste of space," Cerulean said, still laughing. Who the hell are you, but a collection of trash compiled by idiots who do nothing but squawk all the damn time?" Everyone went silent. "You're worse than them. They at least get to be toxic with each other. You're all alone."

"Guys," Gold said.

"Shut up, you unfunny, waste of breath," Cerulean commanded. He wasn't laughing anymore. "I'm so sick of all of you." Everyone stood up slowly. Cerulean turned to Merlot. "You aren't tough. You're the weakest one here. Puff your chest out all you want; we all know that behind that is a weak little boy. Mad at the world because you can't understand it. Mad at yourself because you feel like you should be getting it. Mad at everyone because you think they know a secret you don't. Mad because you aren't the center of attention. Mad that when the attention is on you, you have nothing of substance to say. You should have just died back there."

He turned to Gold. "You want to make people laugh because if they are laughing with you, they won't laugh *at* you. But everyone is just laughing at you. Everyone is looking at you like you're a clown. No one knows who you are. No one wants to know who you are. Everyone just wants to laugh at a joke. You think you understand life's joke. *You* are life's joke, and you clearly don't understand yourself. Though...you are in good company, but you're too busy performing to get that."

He turned to Quartz. "Then there's you." His tone started to imitate Quartz's. "Always so sweet and kind to everyone because no one would hate the nice one. That's not true, though, is it? Because you hate yourself. You *disgust* yourself. You go out of your way to make everyone feel special because you don't think you're worth it. You're not, but because of that, you're just a doormat. You don't even like us, but we're more worth it than the you in your head. Because we can hold our own on our own or admit when it's time to be done. You're never done. You're always on. You're always so full of shit." He raised a hand to me. I forgot that I was even there.

"I'll stop you right there," Cerulean said in his normal voice. "I know. Pot calling the kettle black on that one." He rose and walked toward me. I forgot how to move. "You think you're smart, you think you're above it all, you think you're important. You're interchangeable at best and only interchangeable with losers like these."

He looked at the others, and they were frozen. He looked at me and smirked. "Don't you love that you do that? Freeze people out, make them hate you. Everyone you love, everyone who loves you, frozen. They're over you, they feel like shit at the mention of you, they feel like you need to disappear because you're just a cancer on their lives. That black, putrid, coarse energy is just so revolting. You're worse than worthless..." He looked at me, and I started to cry. The color of his eyes was starting to wash out, and what was left behind was a bright gray. "You're harmful. You're a danger to yourself and others. You make no sense. You claim that you want nothing to do with the world, and yet you're addicted to learning about it and telling people about it. Acting like you're better than them, making them feel like they need you. But when you don't know an answer or get it wrong, it's everyone's fault *but* yours...You feel the air getting colder?"

The air *was* getting colder.

"Harder to breathe?"

I wasn't breathing.

"Feel like you're treading water?"

I don't think that I know what that feels like, but the fact that he was chuckling makes me think that he knew that.

"Feel like you're drowning again? Pitiful."

"Pitiful," the three others said.

I finally noticed that their eyes had long faded to white. Their skin had turned blue and formed black patches all throughout their bodies. The air in the room started to choke the life out of me. My skin felt like invisible needles were stabbing all my exposed skin.

"Stagnant," I breathed out; the words were highlighted with a white cloud. Cerulean whipped his head around and saw what the others were becoming. His face just dropped down.

"I-Impossible! O-Only Merlot got t-touched by one," Cerulean stuttered. I could feel my face scrunch up, and I could feel myself clutching both arms hard while I stared at his fearful face. I shuttered hard. "How is this possible?"

"*You* touched them," I muttered.

"I'm not..."

"They used to be us."

"NO...I...I just wanted...Everyone else got to say how they feel."

"But I think it cuts deeper when it comes from you." Cerulean stopped his shuttering and stammering to look at the wall behind the TV. It finally received splashes of blue paint to fill in the rest of the white.

"I'm not special," he said with a *crack* in his voice. I looked down and saw his hand starting to turn blue.

"Cerulean..."

"You should go."

"But..." The three others let out a loud collective screech. They moaned painful-sounding moans. They turned themselves toward me.

"You should go," he said that more somberly but not really
like himself.

Identity

I was trembling and sweating. I stood up, rushed to draw back the dark blue curtain taking the place of the door. I came to an immediate stop at the doorway because the place had become flooded by the Stagnant. I looked behind me and the ones inside the room were headed toward me with scabby hands reached out. I saw no other choice. I pushed past the hundreds of cold bodies like I was swimming through a strong, half-frozen stream until I was out of the house.

Once I got out, I kept running. It took a few seconds of being outside before I took a step, and there was nothing there. I had fallen from the porch and onto a pile of the Stagnant. I propped myself up from one of the bodies. My face was right in the face of one of the Stagnant. It was like mine in the basic sense. There were a lot more scabs on the lips and side of the face. The eyes were sunken, and it was just dark around them. There was wetness coming from the eyes and nose. When I tried to look the body in the eyes, he looked away.

I felt the impact, but I still felt like I was falling. I didn't really try to get up. I lowered myself and let my arms come up, and the best I could hang around the entity I was on. I let my head rest beside his. The Stagnant stopped their moaning. The silence was deafening. I didn't even want to breathe because I was afraid to break the quiet. My eyes started to sting, and I clenched my jaw.

Eventually, I let out a rough sigh that didn't really want to come out. All the Stagnant bodies began to whale and sob. The feeling of falling ended just as I actually fell to the ground.

The Stagnant that I was on turned into black smoke. Several of the bodies started to follow suit and crumble away. As more bodies vanished, incredibly vibrant green grass underneath was revealed.

I looked at the swirling mass of smoke that was the main part of the Stagnant. I got up. I couldn't tell if I was shaking so much because I was cold or concerned. The blue glow inside started to pulsate fast. There was a low rumble cutting through the sobs and whales. The blue glow inside turned into a black glow. The remaining bodies had their blue parts do the same. I felt a shove at my back, and I stumbled forward. I looked back at the Stagnant body that did that and one behind me scratched my arms. They left dozens of burning red lines on my skin.

I got a couple more shoves from various directions. I knew I couldn't stay there, but my feet were only reacting to my body being shoved and scratched. Something in me was fighting leaving. I was tossed around, taking whatever the Stagnant was throwing at me. I closed my eyes, and that amplified the stench in the air. I just accepted this life that I was now living. I thought I deserved it. *But that's not what I want.*

I fell to the ground again. The Stagnant had pushed me out to the street where there were no more bodies. I looked back and saw the copies reaching for me. The low hum had got a lot louder. My heartbeat was a lot louder. My arms were throbbing with pain. All my thoughts were silent for once. The copies inched closer and closer. In a way that I'm sure will make me sound insane, I was okay with this; at least I wasn't opposed to it. My thoughts started to come back into my head, but they were calmer and slower.

You'd get to leave your fear behind.

You'd get to leave your loneliness behind.

You'd get to leave your pain behind.

You'd never be a burden to anyone again.

You'd get to stop.

You'd finally get to do nothing, be nothing, have nothing, just stop.

All I want is to stop.

Wait

Is that true?

That can't be true? That can't be all.

Because why do I hope I can still see Quartz's smile again? And maybe I'd get to see the version with less tiredness attached.

Because why do I hope to hear Gold try and make me laugh? And I think it would be cool to laugh together at something actually entertaining.

Because why do I hope to feel the heat of another Merlot rant? Maybe we'd finally bond if he heard my burn on Gold there.

Stopping can't be the only thing I want because I haven't tasted the sweet success of proving to Cerulean that this waste can survive.

I could smell a stench so bad that it could wake the dead. The Stagnant were on top of me.

If all I was going to do was get this far, sit on the ground, and quit, then what was the point of any of this?

"If you don't want to be Stagnant, you have to make an effort to move," someone said that sounded like me.

It could have come from me, the Stagnant, or somewhere else. I didn't care. They were right. I took the brief moment of clarity and ran with it. I ran from the dark crowd. I ran, and I did not look back. That said, I wasn't sure what I was looking at when I looked forward. The world had changed since I had been at the house.

The sky was black, save for one pure white star shining alone. All I saw before me was a sidewalk lined with pale orange streetlights. Hearing the moans of the Stagnant grow louder behind me, I started running down the path. I ran and ran but only saw darkness and a few feet of the seemingly never-ending sidewalk ahead. Soon, I could only hear my feet hitting the ground and my breath blasting out. I started to slow down. I know I was tired, but whether it was from running or the situation, I wasn't sure. I stopped. I let out one big huff, and I was fine. I tried to think of my next move, but I couldn't. I had just realized that I was never told where I was. I never discovered who or what I was. I was just there on a sidewalk. *That's what I'm thinking about. How selfish of me.* I looked ahead and saw what I thought was an end to the path.

I started walking. The one star in the sky started to get bigger as I walked. I didn't realize how long I was walking or where I was. The star had captured my gaze and didn't let it go. Because of that, I accidentally took a step, and nothing was there. I acted on my instinct to throw myself back, and I landed on my backside with my legs dangling over the edge. I slid back then got on my knees. Peering over the edge I saw boxes with various moving pictures on their faces and glowing with a white hue. The boxes were swirling and falling into nothing.

In one, there was a woman in a blue and white dress. She had long black hair and smooth brown skin and bright brown eyes. She was smiling at a person off-screen. As I focused more on what I was watching, I could hear the image. It sounded like I was in a room with a lot of people murmuring all around. There were a lot of high-pitched clanking sounds and people calling out names of food. The view went from the woman down at a chocolate cake with a scoop of vanilla ice cream.

I heard a young boy's voice thank the woman. After a beat, I heard him say to himself, "One day, she'll be gone." Their vision became blurry. In another, I saw the perspective of someone running around the yard we were all in earlier. The curtains I could see were less dirty, the tree was less full, and none of the plants were as full or thick. But I could smell the sweet wind and almost felt it on my face. I smiled. I shifted my gaze to another image. I saw many children, all wearing either white or blue polos and either khakis or navy pants.

In this perspective, I saw a group of boys pointing and laughing at the person behind the camera. The image got blurry, but a fast and small brown hand wiped the image clear. This person looked around and saw other kids in the distance laughing or looking away. They lingered on a few faces that were trying their best not to look. I felt a tear roll down my cheek, and my fists clenched.

I had to look at another image. The point of view was someone at a dance. There were multicolored lights, people in colorful formal wear dancing, I could hear upbeat electronic music and smell sweat cutting through various strong colognes and perfumes. I liked the song, and so did the person behind the camera. Their view bounced and swayed to the beat. But as their head moved, I saw that they were alone at a big, empty table. They looked down and gathered a piece of cake on their fork. I heard a clatter from something hitting something plastic. The person slammed their hand on the table. Their vision narrowed as they looked around at the multicolored streamers and glowing balloons. They looked over at the dance floor full of people. They looked for a very long time. The more I looked, the more I recognized most of the teenagers as the children from the other image. The ones who made an effort to not look as this person was teased, were now pointing and laughing. I looked at another image.

It was in that room I had just come from. The person was looking at the same static on the television in a dark room. I could hear the same angry voices in the background, but now they were clearer. I could hear a man and a woman screaming about how much they hated each other and calling each other things like "bitch," "worthless," and "lazy." They accused each other of ruining their lives. They both called each other a disgrace. I heard things being thrown. The camera panned down to arms; one of them was bandaged. Each arm took a turn to unwrap the other. Dozens of red scars were etched into the arm. The person shifted and slumped down into a horizontal position. They shifted with discomfort and fiddled with a towel under them. I heard their stomach rumbling loudly. They searched the floor for a very thin blanket and threw it over the top half of their body, which was all that it could cover.

I looked at another image block. There was no light except a single tea candle. I could make out that it was in the same room as the last cube. There were the same people yelling in the background. The person got up and walked through the curtains being used as a door. They were walking through the house. There were a lot more candles everywhere else in the house. The gray carpet was so flat and stiff it might as well have been wood.

Every step produced a creaking sound. There were stains and burn marks everywhere. There was the same ugly mismatched furniture pushed against the walls. There was a wide and tall box television sitting on a bigger, older wooden television with a dial next to the screen. There was a wooden stand in the corner of the room with medals, trophies, and photos of five different children. One of those children, a young boy, looked very familiar. All the awards next to their picture were academic-related.

The person whose view I was observing walked into a dining room with a ceiling fan dangling by duct tape, a dark brown wooden oval table with dingy green felt-covered benches at either side and an unmatching black chair at the head of it. There were five tea candles on the tables. On one of the benches was the woman I saw in the first image. She looked older and more tired. She wore a white bandana over her hair. She looked like she had been wearing her black sweatpants and white shirt for a few days. She was yelling at a man who looked like an older, wider version of the familiar young boy sitting in the black chair. He tried laughing at the yelling through a plastered-on smile but ultimately succumbed to joining in on the screaming match. He looked cleaner in a black polo shirt, khaki shorts, and a digital watch on his wrist. I looked closer and noticed it wasn't even on.

The person passed the woman and man. I could feel myself scrunching into myself. My heartbeat quickened. I hoped that these two wouldn't notice this unfortunate person. The view looked down at a hole in the floor between the unfinished, ugly, off-white tiled floor. They stepped over the hole and arrived in front of a stove that had all burners on high, producing blue flames. The stove's flames illuminated the stove and the counter next to it. The person I was following took a beat-up pot of simmering water and took it back the way they came. They went into a bathroom and poured the water into a roast pot fixed in a seashell-shaped sink. They looked at the floor that had different big white tiles and several blank spots of wood and holes in the floor.

There was a five-gallon jug full of water that the person took the cap off of and carefully poured some into the roast pot. They then lifted the jug to their face. I heard a quick gulp and sigh. They sat the jug down and found a little bit of soap in a dish on the ledge of a stained white tub and a clean towel. I couldn't watch that anymore. My face and the collar of my shirt were soaking wet.

There were several images of the person lying in a hospital bed. Somewhere, they were getting screamed at by the two in the dining room. Somewhere, they were crying alone. Somewhere, they were standing in the rain in front of a dark building. There was one where the person was in a pool looking at their shirt. There was one where a hand was giving the someone behind the camera a giant stuffed white rabbit with a pink bowtie.

In another image, the person was making the same stuffed animal dance for a crying baby. The baby stopped crying, and I heard laughter from the person and the baby. I stopped trying to focus on the boxes and let them swirl and fall into the nothingness. I noticed that the abyss I was peering into was becoming more and more lit. I looked up, and the star was in front of me. It was just as big as me. The light was bright, but it didn't hurt my eyes.

"Hello?" I said.

"We aren't supposed to be here," the star said. It sounded like me, but the voice was deeper with very little inflection.

"Are you lost too?" I asked.

"No," it answered quickly, its voice echoing. "I know I don't belong anywhere. You should too by now."

"Are you Stagnant?"

"I don't have the luxury to be like that."

"What?"

"Never you mind."

"Are you..." I searched my brain for the name the others were saying earlier, but my thoughts were jumbled. "...Inverno?" I eventually asked.

"Inverno is what they called me."

"What *is* your name?"

"I have no name. What is yours?"

"I don't have one either. I guess we're alike."

"We are not alike."

"Right, they named *you*." I wearily laughed.

"We're not alike because you still have hope. You think things will work out."

"I don't know about that anymore."

"Hmmm. I don't buy it."

"What do you mean?"

"No one would go through what you went through for nothing."

My head dropped. I replayed the others, turning into Stagnant in the house. I thought about the Stagnant slashing and pushing me. Everything that happened since I woke up here seemed off, but that was somehow correct. I was dropped in the middle of an awful journey that was reaching the inevitable ending. It felt like I was unnecessarily prolonging a story that should have ended at that house. *Why would I have wanted to carry a torch of pain and suffering knowing I wouldn't make it to the destination?* It felt like that was everything, and nothing at the same time. Like it was just something that happened today, rather than something with reason behind it. I didn't feel anything about that.

"You know what? What's the point? No one cares about me. I can't do anything to make them care. Why do *I* care? Why do I want them here? Do I want them? What is wrong with me? I don't belong in this world. It would be better for everyone if I just vanish."

"Where have I heard that before?"

"Oh, come on!" I blurted. "Do I have nothing that belongs to just me?"

"Why...Why...Why..." the star said. It flashed brighter, and as it faded, it faded to the point where it barely glowed. It had changed its shape to something different. It made itself into another lookalike, but they looked strange. They had white irises, and they were noticeably younger-looking. They had less hair, less weight, and their outfit was a white T-shirt, blue jean shorts, and black sandals. They still floated before me over the abyss. "Why?" it said again, the echo dropped. The voice sounded more like me, *whiny and unsure.*

"Why me?" I didn't know who said that. "Why me? Because I deserve it. I *deserve* it. No one deserves this. No one should take this. I shouldn't be alive. Friends? *What* friends.

Friends betray me. Family? What a joke. Passions? Dead. I can't do anything right. Look at how this ended. Four dead lights and one fading away now. I'm sorry I cursed you with hope just to have someone help me feel *something,* at least not negative. That doesn't make sense. Five lights all fading out until only one remained. The innocent. The naive. I didn't want your story to end that way. I just think it's inevitable. I don't know who you are. I don't know who the other four were, either. I just knew that I needed to see what hope would do for them. Could that be the key to things finally changing?"

"Hope just seems like such a dangerous drug," the star said.

You get hooked on the feeling. You need to keep it going. You do anything to keep it alive. You can be stripped of your dignity, your possessions, your connections, and you just stand there with no common sense but a ton of hope that it all works out. When it doesn't, and you're at the point of no return, the crash isn't something you easily recover from. Some don't. Now, instead of walking blindly with hope in your heart, you just stop moving forward. You can't even regress because what is there to regress to. Naiveté? Ignorance becomes so much less blissful when you become aware of how ignorant you are.

Life just seems like a series of doing things until you die. But since we're all so afraid of the ultimate unknown that is death, people have given themselves the added task of making an impact so big it's like you never died. Legacy is born from fear and hope. When hope dies, there's just fear. When you're numb to fear, you stop moving forward. Maybe this place was better gray and unexciting instead of a few patches of color-stained black.

So what?

"What if it didn't have to be that way?" I said. "What if we had the ability to make ourselves feel better. Maybe just talking to other people about it, getting them to know about it, would make us feel better. I mean, if we had other people know our pain, they'll help us, right? We could help them. We can be a bright spot in their life. All of your light doesn't have to die. We talk about hope like it's a problem to solve. We talk about not moving forward like it's a requirement. We talk about failing as if it's inevitable. But that's not the point. Hope is just hope. We can't always see that it's neither hope nor ignorance that keeps people moving forward. It's because *life* moves forward. Whether we want it to or not, life moves forward. It doesn't wait for you to stop mourning the loss of a loved one; it doesn't pause so you can ask out your crush before the kid you barely know.

"But hate does. It doesn't care if you can't pay your bills. It doesn't care what you've accomplished. It doesn't care if you're alone. It doesn't care if it's directionless. It doesn't stop. So, we make a choice. Take action and move forward, or don't. Hope doesn't move us forward or hold us back. It's what we do with it that gives it significance. That's with anything we ever come into contact with. People don't have hope and live a happier, safer life. They live. If we take every positive emotion that a mind shrouded in darkness can't comprehend and put it on a pedestal, we become less than in our own minds."

It was quiet for a long time. The star began to float away from me. I crawled toward it. I needed to know what it was going to do. I reached out and tried to touch the star, and I ended up coming down on air. I steadied myself in time and stumbled away from the edge. I looked out, and the star was floating above the center of the abyss.

"How much of yourself will you sacrifice?" I heard a familiar sweet voice ask from behind me. I turned, and I saw it was Quartz sitting with his legs crossed. He didn't look Stagnant. I smiled instantly. "What do you care about? How do you quantify that? Do people need you for emotional support? How much of your heart is dedicated to them? Do you have love in your heart? Is that love for everyone or just a few? Is the right thing to hide your feelings to make someone feel better? Are you willing to give all your heart away? Are you okay with that heart breaking and getting rebuilt over and over? What inspires you to smile and bring out the best in someone? What makes your heart bleed?"

"I don't know about any of that anymore," I said. "I think that it's possible to give too much and care too much. If you prioritize everyone else over yourself, then you don't realize that you're not giving yourself a fair chance. If you go so far as to make it a codependence, then you throw yourself in the line of fire, and the person you are protecting doesn't get the chance to learn, grow, and get stronger. You can support without being the main pillar. It's noble to want to be that much of a shield, nurse, and therapist, but when do you get *your* care? Where's all the fight for yourself."

"What's your message to the universe?" I turned to the left, and Gold was sitting there. "The spotlight is on you. Everyone waits with bated breath. What do you say? Don't you crave the attention? Don't you crave the admiration? Don't you wish that when you are around, no one thinks of the bad things going on in the world? Don't you hope that everyone smiles because you made them smile? Isn't that worth not being taken seriously? What's the point of seriousness if it only brings negativity? What's the point of knowing anything if you walk away knowing there's so much you still don't know? What's the point of ice cream cake when it's dry, has no real icing, and is inferior to its components? What makes you happy?"

"You would think after telling someone to put themselves first, I'd have a more personal answer to that question. I haven't done many things, but I know I like to sit and think. I like creativity. I like...generic answers. I like making people smile, too. I don't like being a burden on anyone. I don't like getting serious, but I know we'd never advance with life if we just stayed in a state of silliness and distraction. I'm not the biggest fan of the spotlight. Maybe that's because I don't have the confidence to handle the attention. Perhaps it's because I don't have much to say. Hard to believe, I know. But I want to have something to say. I want to be a part of the conversation and not take away from it. I want to be in on life's joke, not be it."

"Aren't you angry?" Merlot said. I turned, and he was sitting beside me and leaning over. "The world isn't fair. We're treated like garbage because of the way we look, and it's not even a choice we made. Someone hates us just because our skin has a different color. We're treated like idiots for messing up words or giving an unfavorable opinion.

"We live in a world where a life can be taken at any time, with a bullet, blade, rope, or just the wrong word said at the wrong time. But God forbid you go out on your own terms because that's cowardly. If we let ourselves get distracted from the serious topics, that's wrong; if we let the seriousness take us over, that's wrong; if we don't pick a side in all of these insignificant wars on ourselves, we're wrong; no matter what side we pick we're wrong. I get not being a joke, but doesn't it seem like we're just someone's plaything?"

"I don't like being angry. Often, it causes more problems than it solves. More than that, it makes me feel ridiculous for getting angry because I can't solve the problem. It's such a complex and simple issue. It's not that being angry is wrong. I know that much. But I think anger needs to go somewhere. I imagine it's like fuel. As it burns away, you start to understand what you did not previously. I think it helps someone to make an effort or, rather, a new effort. Sometimes, I can't think of why I, or anyone, would show such vulnerability to expose such passionate thoughts in such an aggressive manner. It seems useless.

"But what use is any emotion in communication? What use is any communication in life? On one hand, it's important to communicate to convey your intentions, desires, and connect to others. But if we don't find the right balance of emotion, communication breaks down. It seems pointless and yet important, but also incorrect, but it feels right. Life is frustrating. It's okay to be frustrated. You *should* be frustrated. That frustration means that you can understand that something is wrong. But we can't stop at just knowing there's an issue and not offering anything else."

"Do you think you're clever?" Cerulean was there on the other side of me, leaning back on one of his hands. His tone was as cold as ever, but now it just felt artificial. "Do you throw out a few facts and make a decision that happened to turn out well, and people call you smart? Do they ask you to think for them and make all the difficult choices? Do you just parrot information that everyone has access to, and people refer to you as 'all-knowing?' Even though that infuriates you, do you revel in it a bit? You must. You sit here under the farce that you have the answers to the world when you yourself are new to it.

"When you don't have the real answers to what really matters, then why even pursue knowledge? Power? Validation? Award? A mind may be a terrible thing to waste, but you can't say ignorance isn't bliss and wisdom is folly. Whereof one cannot speak, thereof one must be silent, but he who knows does not speak. He who speaks does not know. An unexamined life is not worth living, but—"

"Stop," I said. I trembled a bit, but I made myself take a deep breath and let it go. There was a delightful warmth from this. I felt like I could say anything to Cerulean, and I rode that feeling. "You're putting yourself on trial for having and sharing thoughts and feeding curiosity. But you're going to have to take the witness stand off the mile-high pedestal. From what I understand, intelligence and wisdom are relative. It's just knowing what society has deemed fact, until enough people doing the research learn more information and accept something else is more correct.

"Demons caused sickness, the sun revolved around the Earth, frosted tips used to be an acceptable hairstyle. Gaining knowledge seems to be the most useful ability, but to be knowledgeable seems to be the most harmful to the mind. You're hated for knowing so much by people who won't bother to try. You hate yourself for learning things you regret learning. You hate yourself for not knowing enough. The unknown consumes your mind, and all you can do is float in the waters.

"You're aware of the isolation, but you can't do much about it without deepening the isolation. You just wish you could go back to ignorance, but then again, you hate that ignorance. You can quote every philosopher, writer, and fan of thinking in the world...at the end of it all, you must choose the path that you want to take. If you want it to mean something, then I think that's worth doing on the terms that you set. Maybe that's how to finally step forward and not just laterally."

"A lot to think about," Cerulean said. Then he smiled. It was big and genuine. I knew that because it made me smile. I looked at the others, and they had the same smiles.

"So..." they all said in unison. "Have you started to find the answer to your question?" My smile faded. I thought about this, and my mind started to do flips. I couldn't look at them anymore.

No...no! What am I? What am I here for? Where do I belong? Someone tell me, and I'll go there and stay. I don't know anything. I don't know my name. I don't know why everyone I meet looks like me. I don't know why I look so weird. I don't know why this cloud of cruel copies is after me.

What am I doing here?

Why haven't I just stopped and let it take me?

Why am I running, and why don't I know where I'm going or what I'm leaving? It has to be better than running and losing everything along the way, right?

Why can't I just stop?

Why'd you give them to me to take them away?

Why'd I have to see that? When am I allowed to be done?

Why is existence on trial?

Would it be this way if I was in a different group?

Did I do something wrong? Did I say something wrong?
Would it be this way if I didn't look like this?
Is there something in me that's wrong or broken?
Can I take it out?
Was I just a mistake?
Is this where mistakes go?
Is this my punishment for something?
I'm sorry. I'm so, so sorry.

Hello? Is anyone even listening to me? Who have I been talking to? How do I fix myself for you? How do I make it better?

Is my skin wrong? Is it supposed to be brown? Is it supposed to be this dark? The images! Some of those kids weren't brown at all, and they seemed happy. Is that right? Can I change this? Is this why I'm not happy? Tell me what to fix! Please! Is it the scars on my body? They're not my fault! At least, most of them aren't. I don't even remember all of them. I'm sorry. Isn't the fact that they burn every time I think of them enough? Are my thoughts burning me as they race by not enough? I can't even think to myself in peace.

Do I deserve this?

"I don't know what I am," I said to no one. "I don't know what I want. I don't know what to think." I stood up and looked down into the void. I felt a tugging on my pant leg. I looked down, and there was a little boy with brown skin, a round face with chubby cheeks, a chunky body, and big bright brown eyes. He wore a stained white shirt tucked into baggy navy pants that were pulled over his stomach with spots of dirt on the knees. On his feet were a pair of silver and baby blue sneakers that were absolutely spotless. His hair was very short and yet very shiny from a lot of oil. I noticed he was clutching an orange lion with a pink, blue, yellow, red, and green mane.

"How do you feel about me?" the boy said.

"I hate you," I felt myself say very casually. I don't know why I said that or why I was smiling about it.

"Me too."

His body started to stretch out. First his legs, then his arms, then his torso. The clothes he was wearing became a very cropped shirt and pants and he busted out of the shoes. A river of hair started flooding down his arms, legs, top lip, and chin. His short hair puffed up and coiled in all sorts of directions. His bright eyes were now dark and hung low with his head. I could see the dark circles and bags under his eyes, old scars on his forearms and legs, his feet were swollen and filthy.

"Wait, don't do that," I said. I held my hands out, but I didn't know what to do. I felt myself struggling to breathe. I'm not sure why; I just knew that was bad. But it was too late. He was my age now. He dropped the lion he had with him. By the time it hit the ground it was filthy and covered in cobwebs and insects. I tried to reach out and dust it off, but the boy kicked it into the abyss. I took my eyes off the boy to see it was too late to save the lion. I looked back at the boy. It was another lookalike wearing a black shirt, black jeans, and black shoes. His eyes were white with a thick black line outlining the iris. Unlike the others I've met that look like me, his eyes were glowing. The glow was a steady pulse, almost like the light was breathing. "Are you...me?"

"You got it," he said; he sounded calm and friendly. "How do we feel today?"

"Confused, tired, frustrated, tired, not that sad anymore, tired."

"Oh? 'Not that sad?'"

"I don't know what I'm doing, but I'm starting to get an idea. I know that's progress, at least."

"That's what they call a breakthrough."

"The breakthrough was realizing that I need to progress, and I shouldn't be afraid of that. I want to just move along and see if there's more to the world."

"As an observer?"

"That's not a swear. It's a steppingstone. I need to know more about where I am and how I fit into this world."

"I think that's enough for this session. I think you did good work today." I looked into his eyes just as they flashed blue. "Thank you for the honesty." He took a hand and shoved me backward. I fell into the dark abyss below. I felt betrayed and unimportant. I felt like I did all of that for nothing. *Is this what life really is? A cycle of disappointment and using people. Am I someone's means to an end? Their entertainment? Is that my purpose? Who was all that for? Are we all just trying to be important? Do we all just hope that instead of being just another piece of debris, we're actually a star?*

What an irrational thought.

***

I speak from knowledge that comes from a lot of experimentation. When I was a kid, if I wanted a new toy for my birthday, I was told to pray for it. Never got anything. When I wanted new clothes of my own, I was told to pray on it. I got pretty good at dressing up rags. If I wanted my parents to chill out for two minutes and stop getting into screaming matches with each other or taking their anger out on me, I was told to just pray for it.

Now, I can't take anyone screaming at me without feeling stung from it for a month. I wanted to not live in a room filled with holes, mold, rats, and have a real bed and real food on a daily basis. I prayed on it, I went hungry on the floor, thinking the rats must eat better than I do. I prayed that all the dark thoughts in my head were just "the Devil talking" and that God would make him stop. I guess you can say the Devil really likes to talk, and God must've had something better to do. I wanted to leave home. I didn't pray, I just left.

One of a million reasons I had to leave, I can recall, is a day I had the audacity to volunteer. I know, I'm so evil. I told her that my volunteer site was in another city; she said okay. I told her it was in another city; she said there would be someone there. I told him that I had a volunteer day in another city, not the school, he said to tell her that. I told her that it was forty-five minutes away, she yelled and said that she got it and not to say it again. With a lump in my throat, I went on about my day.

I went to volunteer the next day, turned down a ride back with other volunteers because I thought I was set and that they would yell if they were on their way for nothing. The phone rang, and she was at the school. I hitchhiked halfway home. It was my fault because I didn't speak up and say anything. It was my fault because I was instructed to do one thing, and a sheet of paper said another. It was my fault we didn't eat for the next few days because all the money went to a neighbor who had to get me and take me the rest of the way. I wasn't a complete degenerate, though; I paid the penance and let her take her anger out on me.

This went on for days. She yelled and pointed. She threw things. She swung hers and didn't apologize for who she hit in the face when she did it. I pointed out what she was doing, and she told me that was my fault, too. That broke me. For the first time, I yelled back and defended myself. She came back harder. She was away from anyone else, so when I realized I was outclassed, I allowed myself to admit defeat. The routine was back to normal.

I no longer wanted to speak. My words were poison. They always were, but I was starting to accept it more. Saying I wasn't that hungry meant that I hurt my mother. Saying that I wanted to go to a different school that offered me a scholarship was rude because that really meant I just wanted to leave the family. Saying that I was sad or angry was taken as just being a brat. Saying I love you meant I wanted something even though I only ever gave. Gave every penny a kid could earn. I can't say I totally meant it, so I guess that one didn't hurt that much. I said they shouldn't smoke and drink away the money, they told me to "stay out of grown folks' business."

I told them something was wrong with me. I told them I didn't understand why I couldn't sleep, didn't feel like doing it, or why I couldn't care about anything. They told me that I needed to stop with the drama. I told a therapist that I was feeling sad. They stopped allowing me to speak to him. I was told to not embarrass the family. As hard as I could, I never found the card he gave me with a number to call him. Silence wasn't any better. Hiding the scars and depression just made me wonder where all the talking for me and the hidden, more digestible interpretations went. Now I was hard to understand and bitter. I was told I was just weird. No, specifically that I wasn't normal.

Friends were all I had. They didn't yell at me, ridicule me, take my money, or even hit me. They didn't resent that I was born. None of them took their anger out on me. I felt like I could be anything, be anyone. There was no one to embarrass. I could explore any side of myself, I could say what was on my mind, I could emote without worrying if I made someone feel like a failure. I was free to do whatever. I loved all my friends. The problem is that I didn't know love had boundaries in these situations. I dumped every problem I had on people. It either pushed them away or gave them the green light to return the favor. We aren't built to handle multiple sets of baggage, at least not without a lot of training and willpower.

So, I ended up giving them the same advice I got in dark times: "Get over it," and I'd want to talk about myself and my problems some more. Plot twist of the millennium: it doesn't work like that. I don't think I've had a healthy friendship that has lasted more than three years.

Wait, if we're talking actually "healthy," let's exaggerate and say a year. Good thing my brain has now built in the defense mechanism of never speaking my mind, or else I'd seriously be in pain. It saved me from calling someone my best friend. It's best to just let my best friend introduce me to *their* best friend and let the jealousy take over. It's more numbing than the embarrassment and obligatory apologies and compliments after. Once I realize I know everything there is to know about them, save for internet history, and they know so little of me, I fade into the background slowly. Actual relationships scare me. It's hard to think of support networks as actual connections of people and not some ancient mythology shrinks spread. My mind can't comprehend the concept of multiple people expressing support for me at one time that's not dependent on something that I have that they need from me.

***

"Okay. I want you to try and relax," a voice said. It was deep, it was slow, it was reassuring, it didn't sound like me. "Focus on the blue light. Breathe deep for me. Let it wash over you like gentle waves. Breathe for me. Feel the vibrations. Breathe. Let it cool your body and mind. Breathe. Let your body relax. Keep breathing. You're doing great. Breathe in and out. Let the machine do its job."

The voice faded.

I couldn't feel my body anymore.

I just let myself fall and breathe.

Life

"Are you okay? Hey! Get up. We have to go!" I heard a voice say. It sounded so familiar. Just as I thought that I realized I couldn't recall where I was. My brain couldn't open my eyes for some reason. I tried, but it was like I was telling someone else's sleeping body to wake up, and they couldn't hear me. Wherever I was, it was cold. I felt my body lying down on hard pavement. I could hear explosions around me.

My body was showered in rushes of competing chilly and warm wind. The air in my ears was both deafening and stinging. Despite that, I heard people shouting. When I forced myself to listen, it sounded more like one person shouting in different voices. The inside of my head felt as if my thoughts had become material, jagged, and were scrambling around.

"Hey! Wake up," the voice said again, or did I say that? It sounded so close to my inner thoughts, but I think someone said it.

I commanded my eyes to open and saw a person looking down on me. He was a man with brown skin, a thick black beard, and a head of short but thicker curly hair. There were round features throughout his face, and he had a round, stocky body. His voice was deep, but there was a light bounce to it. It was like a sweet melody. He wore a pink shirt with a red pocket on the right side under a yellow opened button-down with black shoulders and buttons. He also had on gray jeans and pink running shoes. I took notice but couldn't tell if this was strange or not, but the color of his eyes was pink. *Have I seen that before?*

"You had us worried," they said.

"Speak for yourself, Rosewood," an angry voice said.

I was confused because it sounded like the first person but rough and intense. I looked and there stood a man who looked exactly like the one with the pink eyes except his were red. He wore a red polo shirt, black jeans, and black and red running shoes.

"Could we not start today, Brick?" the pink-eyed man said; apparently, his name is Rosewood.

"If we're not starting today, can we watch TV?" a cheery version of the same voice said. I looked in the direction the voice was coming from, and a pair of yellow eyes stared back at me. This version of this person wore a yellow plaid button-down shirt with khaki jeans and black shoes. "I'm really into this environmental show starring an unusual rabbit and his duck friend. There's this whole 'rabbit hunting season' thing going on, and I want to see how it turns out."

"Oh, for fuck's sake, shut up, Canary," the red-eyed man groaned. "Before I turn you into fucking fricassee."

"Do you happen to know what the penalty is for shooting a fricasseeing proxy without a fricasseeing proxy license?"

"Shut the hell up, or you'll never get out of this alive."

"The blasphemy of it all," Canary gasped.

"I guess we're starting," Rosewood said.

"He started it," Brick said.

"Definitely a team effort. If you two put half as much effort into the mission as you did fighting, this world would be so much more tolerable." *There's still the Stagnant, our inevitable deaths, and a whole world of issues it's up to an ill-prepared generation to face, but sure, that's the issue.* "Now let's use this time to speak openly about how we feel."

"I hate his need for attention." Brick said. *You hate that he gets and owns the attention.*

"I love the attention you give." Canary said with a sultry voice and a wink. *Liar.*

Wait, weren't their names...?

"Rosewood, Brick, Canary...where are the oth—" I started to say. My thoughts started to muddle. My brain felt like someone had set it ablaze. My vision blurred. I couldn't understand what was happening. My breaths became short, my heart raced, tears ran down my face. My already short breaths abruptly stopped whenever I thought about how I didn't understand what was happening. I felt a hand on my shoulder, and I took in a long, deep breath and let it out slowly. I closed my eyes and saw green take over my vision. I took in another breath and let it stream out, and when I opened my eyes, the green turned blue. I blinked, and my vision was normal again. My mind, body, and heart relaxed.

"Are you okay, Lagoon?" Rosewood asked. His hand was on my shoulder. He straightened up my teal button-down and dusted my faded blue jeans with his hand. He pulled the legs of my jeans up, revealing white and green shoes. I shook him away, and he let my pant legs fall.

"I'm fine," I—Lagoon said. He stood up, and I looked at the blue sky. I—he felt nothing. "I think I just comprehended something," Lagoon said. "Goodbye."

"What?"

"We should get moving."

"Why?" Canary asked. "It's not like the world is ending any time soon."

"Sure," Lagoon said. Without looking back at him, he started walking off. The other three looked at each other and followed him. "I just want to see a better, or at least *new*, ending."

***

Is there a point, or is there no point? There may be a point in combing your hair. Maybe it's to look good for a job interview. The point of that could be to land a job. The point of that would probably be to earn money. The point of having money is to buy the things we need to survive. The obvious point of that would be to survive. But why do we survive? Well, the opposite would be to perish, and I won't even pretend like that isn't a scary thought. But we all die eventually anyway. Death happens no matter what, so why do we bother?

Question, who invented the word "butt?" No, seriously, stay with me on this journey. You could probably tell me the etymology dating back to the first recorded usage of the root of the word, but maybe not the first person to say "butt." Not the person to make 'butt' popular. Definitely not the first foreigner to come into town and hear it and spread it around.

Someone looked at a posterior one day and said, "We should call that a butt." Or even, "those are buttocks, or 'butt' for short." Why? Maybe it was to keep their perversions secret, so they needed a code word for a person's backside. Maybe they thought it sounded funny. Maybe no one wanted to say the whole word. Someone thought of it. We still use it today, and pretty commonly. Yet, no one can tell me the name of the person who first said it or, at the very least, got other people saying it. A name lost in the wind. Sad, yet so common. Legacy is such an important thing for humans to set up before death, but ultimately, it doesn't happen the way it's planned. People are forgotten and misremembered. Though, at the same time, there *was* an impact. Despite people not knowing who you are, your actions made an impact. Your choices had an influence.

Stories are told wrong sometimes. Details get left out, influenced by emotion, or altered to make it more palatable. People don't always get the credit they deserve. It's the impact of the story, however, that I care about. I think a lot of people feel that way. What do you get from the story? What's the message the author needs me to know? Is it a warning? Should I only follow the rules? Should I break the rules? Can humans be trusted to make good decisions on their own? What would I do for love? Is revenge justifiable? Am I just killing time? What is the point? I think *you're* the point.

The "story" was put out into the world with the reader or listener in mind. You sat through it to see where it went. Then we ask, "What's it all mean?" It's *you*. You're the reason it's there. You make the argument of the point beyond that because your interpretation is yours. You tell the story, retell the story, alter it to fit your ideas, to discover what you need from it. When the original author is dead, they may have said their intentions, but in years to come, they will be ignored. Their story and their life will be up for fresh interpretation.

Would a star exist if humans weren't there to look at them? Of course. But because humans are humans, they look at them and ogle over their beauty, wonder about their story, and assign them value. You can strongly guide a stranger's thinking with words and actions, but you don't have a say once you're dead. So, we're back to asking what the point is. If it's going to get to the final destination regardless of what you do, you might as well enjoy the ride. Tell a few stories, enjoy some meaninglessness in the form of picture-worthy food, thrills, companionship, enjoy what you want, and leave when nature takes its course.

There are people and pills in the world that do nothing but try and help you enjoy the ride, might as well use them if you need them. It's really your choice. Your interpretation. With your experiences influencing it later. Make your own story, do your own work, let's see what means something to you. If you hate the story that you're in, start a new chapter, change the setting, find a new character.

Is it really living if your story is in the hands of those who witness it and retell it as they see fit? Why make your actions known if someone changes the meaning of them? Why share your thoughts if others will just distort them? Why learn if it ends with you knowing that you know nothing? Why interact when someone might confuse that with pushing away? Why even be if just doing nothing but existing can offend someone? Because life goes on anyway, and your suffering won't change that. On the other hand, your happiness can make you not think about anything else not close to your heart.

You're here. Life has joys, and life has sorrow. Maybe the secret of it all is to live for joy and suffer through the sorrows to make joy even better. Maybe the point of humanity is to just write a good story for someone to read, retell, and maybe try to top. Create your better ending. The second you are born; you start to die. So why live?

You live because you will die, and the happiness you find along the way is an amazing distraction.

***

Afterword

So that was a lot.

I told you; my inner voice never shuts up.

Sometimes I hate it, sometimes I'm terrified of losing it, and sometimes it was all that keeps me going. When you grow up lonely and you've been sick of yourself since you were five years old, the voice morphs. It's still you, but it says things that you can disagree with, go back and forth, they become a version of you from another perspective. Before you armchair psychologist me, think of the last argument you acted out in the shower. Think about all the hypothetical arguments that you have and hopefully win because it's *you*. You're thinking in another perspective as another person. So, when I'm done having a back and forth with the policy makers at my job that only exist in my head, I look to myself for comfort, reason, a laugh, or support in my rage.

Now that I have adult money, I mostly spend it on chocolate, tacos, therapy and prescriptions. That works for me. I knew therapy and pills wouldn't change me; it's not necessarily supposed to. But I enjoyed spending forty-five minutes to a rare hour feeling validated when I said I wasn't OK. I felt lighter when all the darkness I've had in my life spilled out. This is by no means an endorsement of anything. For every good therapist/counselor that I've had (shout out to Jeff), I've had one that makes me wonder if the universe even wanted me alive. It took a while to realize that I pushed on just to spite that thought. "Be stubborn and live in spite of the world" isn't really a catchy positive slogan to put in PSAs about mental health, would have helped me in school.

When I attended Eastern Michigan University, I submitted a lot of dark writing to my Creative Writing professors. At first, I told myself I was just trying something new and challenging myself to stray from comedy. As time went on, dark just became the norm. As I went day after day with depression and self-isolation, I just let it all out on the page. Sometimes it was a cry for help, sometimes I didn't even think what I wrote was anything shocking or depressing (though it was). To end the Creative Writing Program, you must complete one final class where you work on one final project.

On my bookshelf is a copy of a book called *Dead Light*. Purchased just hours before I needed to turn it in, I received from Kinko's a spiral bound, about 10,000-word, embarrassment. Complete with a stolen, blurry JPEG of space on the cover and no page numbers because I had no time for that. This was the final project I submitted to the Creative Writing program. Three years of rewrites, denouncing the project and coming back to it, here we are. Getting my thoughts on the page made me feel, and feeling was what I needed. To anyone asking if journaling was ever on the table: Nope.

I hope you enjoyed a look into my madness.

Chromotherapy
By Jarron Blake

About the Author

Jarron Blake is an author and ghostwriter living in Ypsilanti, Michigan. Jarron has spent most of his adult life fighting against food insecurity in his community or ghostwriting for others. Now, Jarron is ready to share his writing with the world. When he is not writing, you can find him watching critiques of TV and film on YouTube, painting, or taking extremely long walks.

Read more at https://www.jarronblake.weebly.com.